THE GREAT TOBACCO CONSPIRACY
A Star Original

. . . There was the crack of a distant rifle shot. Simultaneously, one of the living room windows shattered. Shards of glass flew into the room.

'Down on the floor – quick! Snowey – the lights.'

Quickly, Barton took command of the situation. He pushed Virginia to the floor, and threw himself down beside her. In the meantime Snowey had crossed the room in two strides and snapped off the electric light switch.

'What was that?' Virginia was in total confusion.

Barton's voice was firm: 'Our old friend the three-o-three, if I'm not mistaken.'

As if to confirm this deduction, another shot cracked. Glass littered the room once again.

Barton spoke from his position on the floor. 'This fellow is getting beyond a joke. Snowey – get the door open and get into the lift. I'll be right behind you. We'll see who it is taking pot shots at us.'

DICK BARTON – SPECIAL AGENT

No. 1
THE GREAT TOBACCO CONSPIRACY

Mike Dorrell

A STAR BOOK

published by
the Paperback Division of
W. H. ALLEN & Co. Ltd

A Star Book
Published in 1978
by the Paperback Division of
W. H. Allen & Co. Ltd
A Howard and Wyndham Company
44 Hill Street, London W1X 8LB

Cover photo shows Tony Vogel and Anthony Heaton in a scene
from DICK BARTON – SPECIAL AGENT, a Southern Tele-
vision Production, in association with Demob Ltd

Printed in Great Britain by
Hunt Barnard Printing Ltd, Aylesbury, Bucks

ISBN 0 352 30307 7

Chapter One

Captain Richard Barton, M.C., and Sergeant George White, better known as 'Snowey', both now demobbed from the commandos, prepare for an evening out and come across more excitement than they bargain for.
Now read on ...

The War was over. Hitler had spent his last days in the bunker, V.E. Day had come and gone. The new Labour Government had just come into power. The blackout had ended, but rationing continued. Lend Lease was ending and, as the Americans withdrew their money, it was slowly dawning upon some of the British people that the battle was not yet over.

In the living room of a select flat in Chelsea, Snowey White, ex-commando, who had spent four years in full combat kit, was now struggling to fit himself into a full set of evening clothes. He was having trouble tying his bow tie. It was not an object that he was used to wearing. Etiquette had never been one of Snowey's strong points. He had preferred to leave questions like that to his superior officer, Captain Dick Barton.

As Snowey struggled with the ends of the tie Barton came into the room.

'Sir,' said Snowey.

Barton slipped easily into his dinner jacket. He donned urbanity as easily as he slipped into a landing craft on a dark night on a beach in Normandy.

'What's up, Snowey?'

Snowey took his hands away from his collar in disgust. His hard face wrinkled. He would obviously have been happier with his muffler. 'This blooming tie, sir. Or rather

5

it ain't up. I can't do nothing with it. Peculiar sort of object.'

Barton suppressed a slight grin. Snowey had his good points; more than once during their four years together he had proved his worth. But dressing up for an evening out had never been his forte. Unless it was going out on a night patrol.

'Let's give you a hand,' Barton said. He crossed the room and deftly began to tie the knot in Snowey's tie.

'I mean it's all very fine and large, sir,' Snowey complained. 'But I don't see no call to go dressing ourselves up in monkey suits.'

For a moment, Barton was silent. His face creased as he concentrated on the knot. Like everything he did, it had to be perfect.

'We're going on the town, Snowey. We've both been in the dumps, you know that, since we were demobbed.'

Snowey thought about the wide lapelled pin-striped suit that he'd sold to his cousin down the street. About trying to settle down to his old job and finding that he couldn't. 'True enough, sir. Civvy Street seems a bit tame after four years in commandos.'

'Right,' Barton replied. He meant what he said. He was getting bored with hanging around his flat all day. Things had a jaded air about them. Excitement was lacking. 'So, tonight we're going to have a bit of excitement,' he said. 'Rex Marley's singing at the Blue Parrot.'

Snowey had trouble keeping still while Barton tied his tie. Didn't even know what it was all about anyway. 'Rex Marley, sir?'

Barton stepped back for a moment. A frown creased his face. He spoke a little sharply. 'I wish you'd drop this "sir" business, Snowey. I'm not Captain Barton any longer – and you're not Sergeant White.'

Snowey remembered one particular dawn in a small village outside Paris. Barton had pulled him out of the middle of a minefield. He'd been chasing a chicken. 'I keep forgetting,' he muttered.

Barton began work on the tie again. 'You don't forget Rex Marley, though, surely. You were quite a fan of his as I recall – had a couple of his records.'

6

It had been before the War. Before things had changed. It seemed a long time ago. Before Glen Miller had gone missing.

'Oh – Rex Marley, the crooner, sir. Sorry, I'll never get used to not calling you sir, sir.'

Barton grinned. He knew what Snowey meant. In the years they had been together they had become a team. It seemed impossible that their relationship should change. 'We saw him a couple of times with ENSA,' Barton said.

'Every night something awful,' Snowey said. He meant it. Give him a good line of chorus girls any day. Even Vera Lynn or Anne Shelton, before some of the routines they'd passed off on them as entertainment.

'They did a good job, Snowey, and don't you forget it,' Barton said as he put the finishing touches to the knot. The result was a perfect bow with the knot exactly centred. 'Even if some of them weren't up to West End standards. But Rex Marley's in a class of his own. There,' He finished; and as the job was completed, he stepped back.

Snowey walked over to the mirror to examine the new image. He looked as if he still wasn't sure that he approved.

Barton spoke to his ex-Sergeant as he watched him making faces at himself in the mirror.

'So just slip on your jacket and we'll be off for the night of our lives!'

A discreet blue neon light in the shape of a parrot shone at the end of the Mayfair mews. Parked on the cobbles underneath the light was the sleek shape of Dick Barton's Riley. The engine ticked over slowly underneath the reflection of the Blue Parrot. It had the soft purr that indicated perfect maintenance.

Inside, sitting on the soft leather front seat, Snowey White fiddled with his bow-tie as he waited for Dick Barton to speak. He had just asked his ex-captain about how he happened to know the crooner, Rex Marley.

'Of course, I knew Rex before the war,' Barton replied. 'Before he became a crooner, even. His father owns International Engineering, the firm I worked for, and poor old Rex had been stuck in the drawing office. But it was never

7

for him. Eventually, he broke away and did what he really wanted to do.'

'This crooning?' Snowey began to open the car door.

'Right.' Barton switched off the ignition and the Riley's engine died. 'One of the best, though, old Rex.'

They walked towards the Blue Parrot in silence. Their footsteps echoed across the street. The entrance was a small blue door that opened on to a steep flight of steps. The recessed lighting showed them the way down.

The main room was small, with tables scattered around three sides of the tiny dance floor. Through the dim light and the suggestion of a smoke haze, Barton could see a trio consisting of bass, piano and guitar. They were playing 'I Fall in Love Too Easily' – the Frank Sinatra hit from *Anchors Away*.

Luigi, the head waiter, whom Barton had known in the pre-war years, crossed the floor towards them. He said good evening deferentially. Then, as Barton nodded, he led them to a table just in front of the small stage.

'There, Mr Barton. The best table in the house for you.'

'Thanks, Luigi.'

Barton settled into one of the chairs at the table. Snowey followed more slowly. The ex-sergeant, on his first visit to a Mayfair night spot, looked around the Blue Parrot. He was impressed.

'This is a bit of all right, sir.'

'Not bad, eh?' Dick Barton smiled. He looked up on the stage but there was no sign of Rex yet. He thought he could detect a slight tremor of nervousness in the way they played. Almost as if they were making the number last too long. But it was nothing.

'Young Dick Barton, by all that's holy!'

The interruption startled the ex-captain. He had not expected the familiar voice in these surroundings. He turned around to see the distinguished looking gentleman advancing on them. He had no difficulty in recognising his employer, Sir Richard Marley.

'Sir Richard. This is a pleasant surprise,' Barton said as he took his boss's hand.

The older man gripped Barton's hand warmly. There was a firmness about his grip and yet Barton thought he was looking for something. Perhaps it was confirmation.

'Mutual, I assure you.' Sir Richard's deep voice echoed around the room. 'I don't think you know my daughter Virginia?'

Barton had to admit his attention had been wandering during the handshake. He couldn't help but admire the tall, attractive girl that had stood silent behind his former employer.

"I remember a schoolgirl in a panama hat and a gym-slip of that name.' His gallantry didn't fail him.

'Hello, Mr Barton.' Virginia smiled at him. It was a straightforward gesture.

Barton looked keenly at the girl. For once he had to admit that his memory had played tricks on him. It was unusual.

'You've grown up,' he said. They looked at each other, exchanging confidences.

His interest was too much for Virginia. She blushed. Barton thought it was becoming.

'Thank you,' she said demurely.

Barton turned to Snowey who was already rising from his seat at the small table. 'This is my friend Mr White.'

Dick Barton made the introductions with his usual aplomb. But he had never been one to miss out on the urgency behind the apparent social graces and he was therefore not surprised when Sir Richard said: 'Still not made up your mind, Dick? About coming back to your old job?'

It was an inevitable question. One which Barton had not delayed asking himself. His only trouble was with the answer. Frankly he couldn't see himself returning to International Engineering. Not after the war he'd had. Civvy Street didn't seem to be his line any more. 'I'd like a week or two, sir, to think about it.'

Sir Richard had enough respect for his former – and potential – employee not to press the point. 'Well . . . I'm keeping it open for you.' He gestured towards his daughter who had been standing beside him, and, it seemed to Barton, becoming increasingly agitated as the moments passed. 'Come along, Virginia, better get to our table before your brother starts his turn. A prospect I view, I must admit, with mixed emotions.'

As Sir Richard, owner of International Engineering, and a regular attender at the House, started to move away, his daughter lingered. One look into her eyes told Barton that she was troubled, that she was not stopping to arrange a tête a tête with him. Whatever it was, was far more important.

'Mr Barton,' Virginia whispered. Her voice was urgent. 'I must talk to you. It's about Rex. I'm dreadfully worried about him.'

A frown crossed Barton's intelligent face, though he tried to keep the expression from his voice. To maintain a neutral tone in the face of possible trouble.

'Worried, why?'

Virginia glanced towards her retreating father. He was waiting for her. 'I'll tell you when we can talk,' she replied. 'It's difficult here.' Her tone became even more anxious. 'Can I come and see you?'

'Of course.' Barton kept his voice casual. 'I'm in the book.'

'Thanks.'

And so Virginia Marley, ex-schoolgirl who had graduated to evening dress in a smokey West End club, hurried after her father. Barton sat down again.

'She seems in a right old two-and-eight, sir.'

Snowey echoed what had been precisely Barton's thoughts a minute or two earlier. That was why they had made a good team. And still had the potential. 'Yes,' he said thoughtfully. 'Yes, she does, doesn't she?'

Even as he spoke there was a roll of drums from on-stage. The sound filled the small room. The cymbals crashed, and the manager, in evening dress, appeared in the spotlight that had been focused on the centre of the stage.

'And now, ladies and gentlemen, it's cabaret time at the Blue Parrot. For one week only we've been fortunate enough to secure the services of that star of stage, screen and radio, Mr Rex Marley.'

The manager looked expectantly towards the wings and began to clap his hands in spontaneous applause with the

10

rest of the audience. The trio had struck up the opening bars of Marley's signature tune. They added a few more bars. The crooner failed to appear. Slowly, the applause petered out. In the embarrassed silence, Barton glanced across the table to Snowey. His former sergeant shrugged.

'Mr Rex Marley.' This time the manager's voice was obviously anxious.

Across the room, Barton could see that Virginia was on her feet. Her face had a ghastly pallor. Her hand was at her mouth, and she was staring intently at the stage.

The moments ticked by. Virginia's increasing concern was noticeable. At last, Rex Marley appeared from the wings. But, even as he took his first hesitant steps across the small platform, Barton could tell that everything was far from normal. There was a glazed look in the crooner's eyes, he walked as if he was at one remove from himself, in a kind of dream. And, as the applause started up again, Marley looked towards the audience. Startled, as if he didn't expect them to be there.

Softly, Barton said, 'There's something seriously amiss here, Snowey.'

'He doesn't look none too grand, does he sir?'

Carefully, the crooner walked towards the microphone, and the band began to play his signature tune. The manager, after glancing worriedly at the singer, hurried into the wings. The few bars of the introduction over, Rex Marley missed his cue. He came in too late. Worse was to follow; though his voice was confident enough at the beginning, he was soon badly out of tune.

Across the room, Dick Barton saw Virginia get up hurriedly from the table and holding a handkerchief to her mouth, she hurried across the room. Her brother was still faltering on stage, as with one last glance at the singer, Barton got up and went after Virginia.

He found her, face to the wall, sobbing into her handkerchief, in a small corridor outside the main room of the club. As he walked towards her, she seemed not to notice him. He stood there silently. The moments passed.

'Virginia.'

She whirled around, startled. Her face was even whiter than it had seemed a few minutes earlier. She threw her-

11

self into his arms, her sobbing grew worse.

'Oh, Mr Barton.'

Once more, he kept his voice as reassuring as possible. 'Now then young lady – what's all this about, eh?'

The words came between the tears. Her distress was evident. 'I don't know. That's the awful thing, I just don't know.'

Virginia released her arms from around him. She was still holding the handkerchief. She started to dab her face. Tears had stained her make-up. 'It all seemed to start when he came back from his last tour.'

Barton's reply was quick and incisive. 'Where was he touring?'

Slowly, Virginia began to recover her composure. She had stopped sobbing. Her voice recovered some of its former steadiness. 'The Middle East. Egypt, Aden, Palestine.' She paused. 'When he came back he was – I don't know – different.'

'In what way?' Barton asked.

Virginia was an intelligent girl. She could take his questioning.

'Well.' He saw the trace of a smile on her face as she remembered old times. 'You know what a jolly man he was, Mr Barton.'

'Indeed I do.'

Virginia's voice grew more serious. 'He seems depressed all the time now – no, depressed is the wrong word – it's as if he's in a dream all the time.'

Barton had a grave expression on his face. 'I see.'

'He sleeps all day,' the girl continued. 'Sometimes he gets into terrible rages . . . I don't know.'

'Not drinking at all, is he?' Everything had to be considered.

Virginia was suddenly adamant. Her loyalty to her brother was strong, whatever he might have become involved in. 'He never touches strong drink. Never!'

As she finished speaking, the door into the corridor opened and Snowey came out. From inside the club, Marley's voice could just be heard above a series of boos and catcalls from the audience. For Virginia's sake, Barton was glad to see that Snowey had shut the door quickly.

12

'What's happening in there?' Barton asked his companion.

'You heard for yourself.' Snowey, as always, was matter of fact. 'They're giving him a fair old pasting and no error – begging your pardon, Miss Marley.'

'Leave this to me,' Barton said crisply as he strode down the corridor, and pushed open the swing doors at the end. Virginia turned to Snowey. Her expression was one of alarm.

'Never you mind, Miss.' His cockney commonsense came through. His confidence in his ex-captain was apparent. 'Mr Barton'll straighten this out in two shakes of a lamb's tail, never you fear.'

As he opened the door which led to the backstage of the Blue Parrot Dick Barton heard Sam, the manager, shouting angrily at the crooner. From the stage itself came the sound of the trio playing a fast, loud number. He didn't recognise it. He was more interested in what Sam was saying. He crossed the small space.

' . . . You think I pay you a fortune for you to come here and make me a laughing stock? You're fired, Marley – do you hear? Fired.'

'All right Sam,' Barton said, as he saw that Rex Marley could hardly stand. He had one arm outstretched in front of him to brace himself against the far wall. But he was still swaying. His face was tight and drawn. 'Can't you see that he's a sick man?' Barton finished.

'Sick? He's drunk! I'm sorry, Mr Barton, but facts are facts and . . . '

At that very moment, as if to confirm Barton's worst fears about his diagnosis of the situation, Rex Marley passed out. His body went rigid and he pitched forward, unconscious. Quickly, Barton closed the gap between himself and the falling man, managing to catch him under the arms and break his fall.

'Snowey,' Barton called as he took the weight. 'Quick!'

Almost immediately, the door burst open and Snowey, followed by Virginia, hurried in.

'Here I am, sir.'

13

Barton wasted no time. 'Get Mr Marley into my car, Snowey.'

Snowey hoisted Rex Marley from Barton's arms, and began to carry him towards the door as Virginia, almost beside herself, called out, 'What's happened? What's happened?' Her voice had regained its earlier alarm.

Sam turned towards her. He was still angry. 'Your brother's made a complete and utter fool of me, that's what's happened!'

'That's enough of that!' Barton said sharply, as he turned towards the door. 'I'll get his things from the dressing-room.' And with that he went off, leaving Virginia Marley looking into the rather shamefaced eyes of Sam, the Blue Parrot's manager.

Later, sitting in the passenger seat of Dick Barton's Riley as he drove quickly through the West End, Virginia felt slightly better. At least someone competent was now in command of the situation. And for the time being, her brother was safe, in the back of the car with Snowey. But he was still unconscious.

'Where are we going?' Virginia's voice broke the silence.

Barton spoke crisply. His attention did not wander from the road. 'We're taking him back to my flat. He's in no state to be left on his own. And I don't suppose your father . . . ' he left the question unfinished.

'Daddy and Rex don't really get on,' Virginia explained.

Again, Barton's voice filled the small space between them. 'I'd assumed as much,' he said. And then more carefully. 'Rex needs careful watching for a week or two.'

Virginia looked curiously at the ex-captain. He obviously had possession of some information about Rex that she herself lacked. She wondered what it was. But there was no time for questions. Silently, the Riley cut through the London streets. The speedometer flickered upwards.

The front door of Dick Barton's Chelsea flat opened, and Barton and Snowey, supporting the semi-conscious Rex Marley between them, came into the hall. Virginia followed a moment later. She shut the door and switched on the light.

Barton said as he looked at Rex while carrying him down the hall: 'It's beddy-byes for you, my lad.'

Virginia watched them take her brother towards what was obviously Barton's bedroom. She admired the way they handled the matter.

'He's as light as a feather, ain't he, sir?' Snowey's voice echoed down the corridor towards Virginia.

'Yes,' Barton said sombrely. He didn't like the look of things one bit. 'I'd say he's lost a lot of weight since I last saw him.'

Between them, they managed to open the door to Dick Barton's room, and carry the still unconscious Marley over to the bed in the far corner of the room. Then they lowered him on to the bed.

'Just get his shoes off, Snowey,' Barton said. 'I'll loosen his tie.'

As Snowey busied himself at the foot of the bed, Barton looked at the face of his friend as he worked. It was a grim business. He wondered how he would tell Virginia.

When he had loosened Rex's tie and collar, he stood back from the bed, and helped Snowey spread out the eiderdown that he was already holding. Rex had scarcely moved at all since they had brought him in.

At that moment, Virginia appeared in the doorway. 'Shall I make some tea?' she said. She had recovered her composure. That made things even more difficult.

'Good thinking, Ginny.'

Virginia smiled at him before she disappeared. He stood there, looking down at the prone body under the eiderdown. What had started out as an evening that promised more excitement than usual had turned into something far more sinister. Snowey's puzzled voice brought his speculation to an end. For the moment.

'I'd swear that he'd had a bit too much to drink if it wasn't that he don't smell of booze.'

'No, Snowey,' Barton said slowly. 'Rex Marley never touches ardent spirits, we know that. This is something rather more serious.'

When he had finished speaking, Barton turned on his

15

heel and left the room. Still deep in thought, he crossed over to the fireplace. He hardly noticed when Virginia came in.

'The kettle's on.'

Barton turned towards her. Telling her was going to be difficult. The Virginia he had known was no longer a schoolgirl, but then she could hardly be expected to know of the kind of things that could affect a man in the Middle East.

'This is not going to be very pleasant, Virginia.'

Her answer was immediate and defiant. 'I'm not a child, Mr Barton.'

The ex-captain had no difficulty in recognising that fact. But still, he was going to have to be as tactful as he could. 'No. You're a very plucky young lady, I can see that, but . . .'

Snowey's entrance from the bedroom interrupted his explanation. Barton sensed that, for the moment, even Virginia was glad of the respite. 'Sleeping like a babe, he is, sir.'

'Good,' Barton replied.

Snowey was not aware that he had arrived at a crucial moment. 'Did I hear someone mention a cup of char?' he said. He could do with it after all that hefting.

But he scarcely had a chance to finish his sentence. There was the crack of a distant rifle shot. Simultaneously, one of the living-room windows shattered. Shards of glass flew into the room.

'Down on the floor – quick! Snowey – the lights.'

Quickly, Barton took command of the situation. He pushed Virginia to the floor, and threw himself down beside her. In the meantime Snowey had crossed the room in two strides and snapped off the electric light switch.

'What was that?' Virginia was in total confusion.

Barton's voice was firm: 'Our old friend the three-o-three, if I'm not mistaken.'

As if to confirm this deduction, another shot cracked. Glass littered the room once again.

Barton spoke from his position on the floor. 'This fellow is getting beyond a joke. Snowey – get the door open and get into the lift. I'll be right behind you. We'll see who it is taking pot shots at us.'

'Right you are, sir.' Snowey formed a slow grin. 'I thought we was finished with this sort of caper.'

'Apparently this gentleman has other ideas,' Barton replied.

Crouching, Snowey made his way across the room, and opened the door. Barton followed behind him as he'd promised. Before he went out he turned towards Virginia.

'Stay there, Ginny – and keep your pretty little head down.'

Snowey White burst out of the front door of the mansion buildings. At the outer fringes of a pool of light across the road, he saw the indistinct figure of a man running towards a parked car. The man was carrying a three-o-three.

'Here! You.'

Snowey ran even as he shouted. The car was about a hundred yards away down the street. Good job he'd kept in trim, he thought as he ran towards it. He gained ground, but not enough. The engine was running. The figure threw open the rear door of the car. Even before the door was shut properly, someone had put his foot down on the accelerator, and the vehicle roared away. As the tyres screeched, Snowey stopped in the road to regain his breath. He was still panting when Barton appeared at his elbow.

'Get the number, Snowey?'

'No chance, sir.' Snowey replied between breaths. 'Number plate's covered in mud.'

'An old trick,' Barton said, 'but effective enough.'

They turned towards the house.

When Barton returned to the living-room, Virginia was pacing anxiously up and down. Her earlier unease had now become near-panic. 'Mr Barton,' she said as soon as he appeared. 'I want to know! You must tell me what's wrong with Rex.'

Barton took up his usual stance in front of the fireplace. He turned towards the defiant Virginia. For a long moment, in total silence, he looked at her.

Then, reaching into his pocket, he said: 'When I went to get your brother's things from his dressing room, I noticed this in his ashtray.'

He held up what appeared to be a half-smoked, roughly rolled cigarette.

'A fag end?' Snowey couldn't understand what it was all about. There was nothing particularly odd about it.

'Not quite, Snowey,' Barton said grimly. 'It's what they call in their filthy trade a "reefer".' He turned towards Virginia. 'I'm sorry, but I'm afraid your brother is a dope addict.'

She stared at him, wide-eyed, too horrified to speak.

'Dope?' Snowey questioned. He didn't understand all this.

Barton spoke again. 'Marijuana, Snowey.'

Virginia stared at the reefer. Though she was now grown up, no one had ever taught her how to come to terms with this. Dick Barton looked grim. A reefer.

Can Rex Marley be cured of his addiction and his career saved? Who fired the mysterious shots through Dick Barton's window?

Read the next chapter of Dick Barton – Special Agent.

Chapter Two

Beautiful young Virginia Marley, daughter of millionaire industrialist, Sir Richard Marley, asks Dick Barton for help. Her brother Rex, a well-known crooner, is in trouble. Marley collapses on stage and is taken to Dick's flat. A gunman fires several shots through Barton's window but gets away unidentified. Barton breaks the news to Virginia that her brother is a drug addict . . .

Now read on . . .

'Mari-what, sir?' Snowey didn't quite understand what Barton was on about. He knew about drugs of course, but not the details of what it could do to you.

Barton was still holding the reefer in front of him. 'Hemp, hashish, cannabis, dagga – call it what you will – once in its clutches a man is doomed.' Then with a disgusted expression he threw the reefer into the fireplace. After a moment, he spoke again, 'Unless . . . '

Virginia interrupted him quickly. 'Unless?'

Grimly, Barton related what he knew about hashish: 'Unless he can be physically kept from the stuff for at least two weeks, by which time the craving will have subsided. "Cold Turkey" our American cousins call it.' He paused for a moment to see how Virginia was taking his news. The blind panic that had been in her eyes was now subsiding. Slowly, anger was taking its place. 'It's not pretty, I'm afraid, but it's effective.'

'But Rex would never take drugs.' Virginia resisted Barton's pronouncement. She was having difficulty in believing that Rex could fall so low. He had unconventional tastes in music, it was true. At least as far as her father's generation had been concerned. But then the war had changed so much.

'Perhaps unknowingly,' Barton's voice interrupted Virginia's thoughts, 'but the devil's behind this business – and it's a very big business indeed – it will stop at nothing to gain a new recruit to their hideous ranks. How poor Rex was sucked in, and by whom, is what we have to find out.'

Snowey had been listening carefully while his ex-captain spoke. He didn't like the smell of any of it. 'I don't know about big business, sir,' he said. 'It sounds a very dirty business.'

'Indeed it is, Snowey. The dirtiest going.' Just how dirty Dick Barton was not quite sure. But he meant to find out, even if it meant taking up combat stations again.

Virginia Marley felt quite at a loss. What had started out as bewildering behaviour on Rex's part was turning out to have sinister implications. 'But I don't . . . '

Smiling, Dick Barton interrupted her. 'That's quite enough questions for tonight, young lady.'

'I'm not a child, Mr Barton,' Virginia said. She was

determined to find out what had happened to Rex. She wondered if all this 'reefer' business was true. But it must be, if Dick Barton said so. Her father had always trusted him. Even now Sir Richard wanted Barton back in International Engineering.'

'You're a very beautiful young lady,' Barton said gallantly to Virginia. 'And I'm going to claim the honour of driving you home.' Like the gentleman he was, he picked up the fur coat that was lying on the settee, and placed it around her shoulders.

Snowey watched them, wondering what the governor had in mind for him for the rest of the evening. A spot more baby sitting probably. Still, it was easier than looking after an anti-tank position.

As if to confirm Snowey's suspicions, Barton turned towards him. 'Snowey, keep an eye on Mr Marley. Don't let him out of this flat.'

He'd been right then. It was okay doke with him. Dick Barton always knew what he was doing. 'Don't you worry about that, sir,' Snowey answered as Barton ushered Virginia to the door.

Barton turned as he opened the door to go out. 'Just remember,' he warned. 'He isn't himself. He'll do anything, literally anything, to get this drug. He'll show great cunning. He may even become violent.'

When Barton and Virginia had left, Snowey walked over to the fireplace. He was puzzled, he still didn't quite understand what this 'marijuana' business was all about. He stooped down and looked at the remains of the reefer in the fireplace. It still looked ordinary enough. But it was dangerous. Carefully, he picked it up, and held it at arm's length. Then, he sniffed at it gingerly. It smelt foul. Quickly, he threw it back into the fireplace where it belonged. Then, he wiped his hand clean on his trousers. He didn't want to become contaminated.

Once more, Virginia sat in the passenger seat of the Riley Monaco. This time though, she knew the awful truth. Her brother was a drug addict. It would take a long time before he would recover again. If he ever did. She sat, thinking to herself, scarcely caring where they were going.

20

'A penny for them.' Barton's voice broke the silence.

'Will Rex get better again, Mr Barton?' Virginia couldn't help but mention what was troubling her.

'Of course he will.' Barton's comforting voice echoed across the interior of the car. 'He'll have to fight – but he's a fighter, I know that.'

But Virginia was still worried. There was one further question that she still had to face. She shifted in her seat: 'I don't know what I shall say to Daddy.'

Without taking his eyes from the road, Barton answered her directly. He never had been one to evade serious issues like this one. 'Tell him Rex is ill.' He thought that, if he could, he would spare Sir Richard from the shock. 'It's not far from the truth, heaven knows.'

Silence descended on them once more as the Riley headed through London towards Virginia's home.

Meanwhile, Snowey White was preparing himself for a quiet evening in Dick Barton's flat. He was sitting in the most comfortable easy chair, with a cup of char at his elbow, and a copy of *The Sporting Life* on his knees. He looked down the list of likely runners, and seeing one that he fancied particularly, licked the pencil stub that he was holding and marked it down.

It was at that moment that the doorbell rang. Snowey wasn't expecting anyone, the governor wouldn't be back for a while yet. Still, he put his paper and pencil down and got up to answer the door.

He saw through the crack in the door. He hadn't known what to expect, but he certainly hadn't been prepared for this. She was a corker. She was dressed in furs so that you could just see her face. She was standing there as cool as you please. She was somewhere around thirty, and she was still beautiful. When she smiled she showed a row of perfect teeth.

'Yes, miss,' Snowey said. He was very polite.

'Mr Barton?' Her voice was husky, mid-European. It only added to her charm.

'He ain't in.'

She began to wave her arms about in a gesture of distress. 'Oh heavens! They told me at the club that my fiancé was here with Mr Barton.'

He still didn't quite understand what she meant: 'Your fiancé, miss?'

Her distress became even more evident. 'Rex Marley, the crooner. They told me that he had been taken ill. I am so worried about Rex recently.'

'He'll be all right, don't you fret, miss.' Snowey was beginning to feel sorry for her.

She stepped closer to him. He could smell her perfume. 'Then he is here?'

'Well,' Snowey replied. He wasn't sure that the governor would like it.

Once more, she smiled at him. 'Can I see him, Mr . . . ?'

'White, miss,' Snowey said as he introduced himself. ' "Snowey," most people call me, though my monniker's George by rights.'

'Snowey,' she said his name like it meant something. 'I must see Rex. I am so desolate at this illness of his.'

He began to open the door wider so that she could come in. 'Well . . . all right, miss. Can't see no harm in that.'

But the words were scarcely out of his mouth before she turned on him. She reached into the muff she was carrying, and, with perfect grace, produced a small automatic pistol which she trained on his heart.

'Now, Mr Snowey White,' her voice was almost a purr. 'I hope you are not going to be a foolish gentleman.'

'Here! What's this?'

Snowey was completely taken by surprise. He had not been expecting her to produce a gun from her muff, and he didn't expect any further developments. So, when a thug in a flat cap and muffler slipped in behind the dream-boat who had turned nasty on him, Snowey didn't even see the cosh that was brought crashing down on his head. The only things on his skyline were stars.

The woman, whose name was Melissa, turned towards the thug with the cosh. 'Good work, Curly,' she said.

Snowey didn't hear a thing.

There was a blurred face in front of him, but nothing was very clear. Things kept swirling about like a figure eight on a night in Battersea Funfair. And then, out of the swirl, from very far away, came a voice.

'Snowey. Snowey.'

Gradually, the figure eight stopped moving and Snowey found himself staring at the familiar close-shaven features of Dick Barton.

'Cor lumme, sir. Somebody dropped the roof on me, I reckon.'

Barton crouched down beside the ex-sergeant. 'What happened, Snowey?'

Snowey managed to struggle to a sitting position. 'I don't rightly know sir,' he managed, 'and that's a fact.' He rubbed his aching head. 'Oh – now I remember – this young lady came to the door.'

Barton's question was to the point: 'What young lady?'

'Said she was Mr Marley's fiancée,' Snowey continued. 'When I let her in she pulls a gun on me.' He stopped speaking for a moment to rub his head again. 'Foreign, she was.'

Dick Barton didn't like the sound of what Snowey had described. He had a nasty suspicion. Quickly, he got to his feet, strode across to the bedroom door, and flung it open.

'Just as I thought,' Barton said. 'The bird has flown.'

Snowey got to his feet and walked across the room. As he looked into the bedroom he felt a right Charlie. There was no sign at all of Rex Marley, crooner and drug addict. 'I'm sorry, Mr Barton,' Snowey said.

'No good crying over spilt milk, Snowey.'

Still, Snowey felt that he had to explain further. He'd never done anything like this before. Not even in France. 'She seemed on the level,' he said. Then there was a pause. 'Apart from the accent.'

'What was she like?' Barton fired staccato questions. 'Describe her.'

'Well . . . ' Snowey tried hard. His head was still aching all over the place. 'She was a bit of all right – dark hair – lot of make-up and that – big fur coat.' He couldn't go any further. 'I dunno.'

Dick Barton's impatience showed. He must try and make Snowey think a bit harder. 'That could describe about fifty thousand women in the metropolis alone,' he began. 'There's nothing else you can think of? No detail, no matter how small?'

The last question seemed to do the trick. Snowey looked at Barton. He became excited. 'Here – wait a minute. There was one thing.' He was remembering better now. 'When she pulled the shooter on me, her fur coat sort of opened a bit and she was wearing a big brooch on her dress. Funny sort of article,' he said with his usual relish. 'Shaped like a Christmas tree.'

'A Christmas tree?' Barton wanted to be sure that Snowey's memory wasn't playing tricks on him.

'Yeah,' Snowey said quickly. 'Only it wasn't.' Words failed him again. 'I was . . . I'll tell you what it was like.' He grappled once more with the description of the thing that he had seen. 'It was like Chinese writing.'

'An ideogram?' Barton wanted Snowey to be more precise.

Snowey made a puzzled expression. 'I dunno about that sir. It was like Chinese writing – you know.'

Barton's face creased thoughtfully. He was trying to make the connections. And the theories that he was coming up with weren't pleasant ones. 'You said the girl was foreign. She wasn't Chinese, was she?'

Snowey was on safer ground now. 'A chink? Oh no sir – not that foreign.'

But Barton's mind was made up. As usual, once he had made a decision he acted on it immediately. And now, especially, there was no time to be lost. 'Come on, Snowey – we've got work to do.' He started to lead the way out of the flat.

Following closely behind, and still with the remnants of a bump where he'd been coshed, Snowey was less enthusiastic. 'Stone the crows sir, we ain't going to China this time of night, are we?'

You could never tell with Dick Barton.

It wasn't China exactly, but it was about the nearest that Dick Barton could get to it. The place was a small, but expensive Chinese restaurant situated off Gerrard Street in Soho. It was one of many places that he had known before the War. The food was usually excellent, and sometimes, the information was good.

Dick Barton was sitting with Snowey and an Oriental

gentleman called Mr Chen at a table in the corner of the Eastern style room. The walls were covered with a heavy red brocade, with gold Chinese dragons embossed on it, and, in the far corner there was a set of brass gongs in a bamboo frame. Nearer, a stick of incense was burning. The perfume, like Mr Chen himself, was totally inscrutable.

The gentleman from the Orient was sitting at the table wearing a long brocade robe and a skull cap. Up to this point, he had said nothing at all.

Dick Barton finished his preliminaries and turned to Snowey. 'Can you draw the brooch for Mr Chen, Snowey?'

Snowey didn't like the place much, he could hardly breathe what with all that incense and stuff. But he followed the leader, as always. 'I don't know about that, sir,' he said. 'I was never much of a hand at this drawing, but I'll have a go.'

Snowey drew a paper table napkin towards him, brought his pencil stub out of his pocket, gave it a lick, and frowning with concentration, carefully made a drawing something like a child would do a Christmas tree. When he had finished he passed it over the table to Mr Chen.

It was a while before the Chinaman spoke. When he did it was with no apparent sign of regret. 'In Chinese this mean nothing.'

'Sure you've got it right, Snowey?' There was no anxiety in Barton's voice, merely the desire to know.

'I think so sir. Let's have a butcher's.' He leant across the table and pulled the napkin back towards him. There was silence for a while as he studied his attempt.

'No – it ain't quite right. Let's have another go.' And, with even more concentration than before, Snowey began again.

After a while, he spoke. He was still apparently not satisfied with his effort. 'No – it ain't quite right. Let's have another go.'

The procedure was repeated.

'It was more . . . one of the sides was different,' he said at last.

'Assymetric?' Barton cut in.

Snowey grinned. 'If that means both sides wasn't the same, that's what it was, sir. Like . . . '

He was trying hard. Once more, he made his attempt at a facsimile of the ideogram.

'There,' Snowey said when he had finished. He pushed the paper across the table to Mr Chen.

The Chinaman stared for a long moment. Not a muscle in his face moved. Eventually, he spoke: 'It like this?'

'Something like that – yes,' Snowey replied. He couldn't do any better.

'It not have one more stroke, like . . . ' Mr Chen left his sentence uncompleted as he drew a horizontal line across the top of the ideogram.

Snowey became very excited. 'Yes! That's it! That's exactly it!'

The moments ticked by silently. Still, Mr Chen said nothing. At last, he moved his eyes from the paper and looked up at Dick Barton. A complete change had come over the Chinaman. From inscrutability, his expression had changed to one of fear.

'I cannot help you, Mr Barton.'

The special agent could not fail to notice the transformation that had come over Mr Chen. 'You don't know what it means?' Even as he spoke, Dick Barton knew that his assumption was not true.

Mr Chen got to his feet. He stood over the table. It was not regret that motivated him. It was terror.

'I'm sorry,' Chen said. 'I cannot help you. I and my family owe you much, Mr Barton – but this, I cannot help you. Please go.' Soundlessly, and very quickly, Mr Chen left the two enquirers sitting at the table.

'Well, well, well.' Even Dick Barton was surprised.

It was Snowey who spoke first. 'Something seems to have upset him, sir, don't it?'

Barton held up the paper napkin and looked at the ideogram. 'To be more precise, Snowey – *this* seems to have upset him.'

Snowey said nothing. He got ready to leave the restaurant.

Dick Barton had scarcely arrived home before the telephone began to ring in his living-room. He picked up the phone and listened intently. It was Sir Richard Marley on the other end of the line. And the news was bad. Turning to Snowey, who had just entered the room behind him he said; 'Come on Snowey. We're off again. Miss Marley has disappeared.'

Less than twenty minutes later Dick Barton and his right-hand man were sitting in the sumptuous study in the Marley home, while Sir Richard, dressed in a silk dressing gown over his pyjamas, was pacing up and down in front of the fireplace while he explained the situation to them. 'I left that night-club soon after the débâcle with my son and came straight home,' Sir Richard said worriedly. 'I had my usual nightcap and then went up to my room. I read for a bit then put the light out – but I couldn't sleep. My mind kept going over and over what happened at the club. To cut a long story short, I got up again, knocked on Virginia's door and found she wasn't in, came down here and telephoned you.'

'I see.' A concerned frown crossed Barton's face. There was even more skulduggery going on than he'd thought. 'And you didn't hear Virginia come in?'

Sir Richard stopped pacing for a moment. 'No – but then I wouldn't – my room is right at the top of the house.'

Barton commented crisply: 'I dropped her here at exactly twelve fifteen – I remember looking at my watch.'

'Did you see her come into the house, sir?' Snowey's question was a good one. He felt he had to make up for the bloomer he'd made earlier in the evening.

'Good point, Snowey,' Barton added. He got up from his chair and stroked his chin. 'No, I didn't as a matter of fact. As I drove off she was just getting her key out of her handbag.'

Snowey didn't want to jump to conclusions. 'So . . . '

'It's quite possible she never came in at all.' Barton finished off the thought that his ex-sergeant had begun.

It was Sir Richard's turn to join in the theorising; 'You mean . . . ' he began.

Dick Barton interrupted once again. 'I don't know yet, Sir Richard. I just don't know. But wait a minute, I've got an idea.'

Snowey smiled when he saw Dick Barton make for the door. He knew all about Barton's famous ideas. He'd had four years of them, and every one had turned out to be a jump ahead of what everyone else was thinking. He saw the look of alarm on Sir Richard's face next, and reckoned he would have to do what he could to reassure him:

Dick Barton came out of the front door of Sir Richard Marley's house and crossed the road to the taxi-rank and cab shelter that was directly opposite. It was a tiny, steam filled place, built of wood and corrugated iron. There was a table in the middle of the room, around which three cabbies, still wearing their caps and mufflers, were sitting.

'Evening chaps,' Barton said briskly. 'Or should I say good morning?'

The cabbie nearest to Barton looked up from the thick bacon sandwich he was tucking into. 'Where do you want to get to, guv?'

'I'm happy enough where I am, thanks. I'm looking for information.' Dick Barton reached into his inside pocket, took out his handsome pigskin wallet, and extracted two pound notes with a flourish 'There's these two crisp one-pound notes for anyone who can provide it.'

More than a murmur of interest passed around the table. The first cabbie who had spoken even put down his sandwich.

'I want to find someone who was on the rank at a quarter past twelve,' Barton continued.

It was a cabbie from the other end of the table who replied. 'Nah – they'd be well gone by now, guv.'

'Never mind,' Barton said. 'Pass it around among your mates. At a quarter past twelve I dropped a young lady off at Sir Richard's house opposite – number thirty-eight. I was driving a black Riley Monaco.'

The one with the sandwich spoke again. His mouth was full. 'What do you want to know then, squire?'

'I want to know what happened to her after I drove off. I left her on the doorstep.'

Barton grinned as cries of 'shame, shame', echoed around the small, steam filled room. 'That's as may be,' he continued. 'But she never went into the house and I want to know why.'

Then, he squeezed past the table and walked over to a

28

small notice board that was screwed on to the wall. Taking a drawing pin from the edge of an advertisement for a tyre firm, he pinned his visiting card to the cork board.

'My card's there,' he pointed out. 'Anybody who saw anything unusual – just give me a ring. Okay? And don't forget that two quid.'

The burly cabbie at the far end of the table replied for the others. 'Right you are, guv. We'll pass it around, eh, lads?'

There were murmurs of approval.

'Right,' Barton said. He turned towards the door. 'Bon appetit, gentlemen.'

'And you, guv,' said the first cabbie. He took the last bite of his sandwich and wiped his hands on his muffler.

In the meantime, in the study of Sir Richard Marley's house, amongst the leather armchairs and the rows of books with real gilt lettering on their spines, Snowey was doing his best to keep his end up. 'But if anyone can find her, sir, Mr Barton can,' he was saying for the umpteenth time. 'I remember when our company was crossing the Rhine . . .'

Dick Barton came in and overheard the last part of Snowey's remarks. 'Now then, Snowey,' he ordered. 'Spare my blushes.'

Turning around to face Barton, Snowey grinned. He was glad to see him back. 'No, give the devil his due, that's what my old mum always says.'

Sir Richard interrupted the friendly banter. His tone was anxious. 'Any luck, Dick?' He was obviously hoping that Barton had solved the mystery.

'Not yet, Sir Richard – but I hope we'll have some leads soon.'

At that point the telephone rang. Even in the heavily furnished room, the tone sounded shrill and menacing.

'Who the dickens can that be at this time of night?' Sir Richard addressed the question to no one in particular. It was obvious that the strain of the events of the last few hours was beginning to show on him, Dick Barton thought.

'Hello, yes.'

While Sir Richard answered, Dick Barton moved to his

side, and motioned to him. His former employer held the phone so that they could both hear the caller's replies. Barton had more than an intuition that all was not well.

When the voice at the other end answered it was not friendly. It was insinuating and foreign, and more than slightly menacing.

'Sir Richard Marley?'

'Speaking.'

'Sir Richard, you will be well advised to stop Dick Barton meddling in my affairs.'

'Who is this?' Sir Richard's tone was outraged. He turned to Barton who gestured to him to calm down.

'My name does not matter,' the voice continued. 'Your daughter is safe and well. If you want her to remain in that condition – call Barton off.'

To Barton's prompting, Sir Richard said: 'How do I know that Virginia's safe?'

The deadly voice spoke again. 'To prove my good faith I will allow you to speak to her. Here.'

There was a terrible silence. Sir Richard exchanged glances with Dick Barton. The Special Agent nodded, and then went across the room to another telephone. Sir Richard was left alone to hear the voice of his daughter.

'Daddy?'

'Virginia! Are you all right?'

'I am all right. I'm at . . . '

Sir Richard heard his daughter give a little cry. And then, suddenly there was no more of Virginia's voice at all.

'Hello? Hello?' Dick Barton's old employer was now shouting down the telephone.

It was the insinuating foreign voice that picked up the conversation again.

'Don't be alarmed, Sir Richard. Virginia has come to no harm, despite her foolishness. Nor will she come to harm as long as my conditions are met.'

'How am I to know that?' Sir Richard demanded.

'You will have to trust me.'

Again, Sir Richard's reply was angry; 'I see no reason for doing that.'

'You have no choice, Sir Richard.'

The owner of International Engineering could no longer contain himself. 'You unutterable swine . . . '

But, even as Sir Richard was shouting down the phone, the line went dead. And if he, or Dick Barton, or particularly Snowey White could have seen the well manicured hand that replaced the receiver on the other end of the line they would have been even more alarmed. For on that hand was a gold ring. And on the ring was an ideogram that tallied exactly with the one that Snowey had drawn with Mr Chen, and which in itself, matched the brooch worn by the foreign woman with the automatic pistol in her muff who had abducted Rex Marley.

What is the meaning of the mysterious Chinese symbol? Why has Virginia Marley been abducted? Will her father abide by the conditions laid down or will Dick Barton continue his search for her and her brother?

Read the next chapter of: Dick Barton – Special Agent.

Chapter Three

Virginia Marley, daughter of millionaire industrialist Sir Richard Marley, has disappeared after having appealed to Dick Barton for help with her brother Rex Marley, the crooner, who has become a drug addict. Sir Richard gets a threatening telephone call warning him to take Barton off the case . . .

Now read on . . .

'He's cut me off.'

Sir Richard Marley stood at his end of the study with the telephone still in his hand and the expression of outrage still on his face.

Meanwhile, at the other end of the room, Dick Barton was doing his best to trace the menacing telephone call

31

that had revealed that Virginia was in the clutches of an unknown enemy. He held up his hand to silence Sir Richard, then he told him what he was doing.

'Yes,' he was saying into the phone. 'I see . . . Barking 0731. Can you give me the address?' The operator was proving to be slightly sticky on this one; she declared that it was against the rules. 'Oh – but rules were meant to be broken, my dear.' Still, she wanted to know what his business was with the caller.

Barton turned to wink at Snowey and Sir Richard. Then, he resumed his conversation: 'Well, let's say it's a rich auntie of mine stranded in the East End and wants me to go and collect her. But the silly old trout forgot to give me the address. You wouldn't want me to be cut off without a shilling, would you?'

Snowey smiled to himself. Trust the governor. Once in Normandy, he'd even convinced the Jerries that they had reinforcements by dragging a load of bushes through the woods after him.

Barton was still talking into the phone. 'Where? W. H. Brattigan and Sons, 103 Old Street, Barking. Got it.' He tried his charm again; 'You're a lovely girl – remind me to send you a pair of nylons.'

Then, he replaced the receiver on the hook, and turned to Snowey. 'Barking, here we come.'

'I'm coming too,' Sir Richard protested.

'You'd be better employed, sir – if you'll forgive me saying so – standing by the phone here in case we have any further calls from our playmates.'

There was no arguing with Dick Barton's decisive tone, Sir Richard could see that. Still, in this instance he didn't mind taking orders from his ex-employee. Barton was the man for the job, that was clear.

'Oh – very well,' Sir Richard muttered.

'Come on, Snowey.'

And with that, they disappeared into the night.

W. H. Brattigan and Sons turned out to be a warehouse premises in an unsalubrious part of Barking. It was part of a complex of Victorian buildings riddled with alleyways, loading bays, and arches that had seen better days.

The Riley Monaco screeched to a halt in front of a brown painted sign with a peeling logo. Barton and Snowey quickly got out of the car clutching their torches.

'You take the back, Snowey.'

It was like being back in the old times, Snowey thought as he set off down an alley-way to the side of the warehouse.

Barton himself started examining the main wooden door which covered most of the front of the building. It was a large affair, with a smaller door set into it. When he pushed the smaller door it swung inwards revealing a pitch black interior.

Dick Barton stood there for a moment, waiting for his eyes to become accustomed to the blackness. It was a trick he'd learnt on night patrol. Then, he squared his shoulders and stepped cautiously over the sill. Inside, it was even blacker than he had expected. After a few steps, he stopped and listened. A scuttling sound came at him through the darkness. He switched on his torch to see a a large rat scuttling between two wooden crates. He switched off his torch again. The brief moment of light had shown him that the whole interior was full of rows of crates.

Slowly, he advanced further into the warehouse. He could feel the dark wooden towers at either side of him. Then, from the far end of the building, he heard footsteps.

'Snowey?'

'Got it in one, guv,' said the friendly voice, as it punctuated the darkness.

'Seen anything?'

'Not a thing, sir.' There was a slight pause. 'Hang on, though, a minute. There's something here.'

The beam from Barton's torch showed Snowey crouching in the aisle between the rows of stacked crates. He appeared to be reaching for something on the ground.

'Look out, Snowey!'

Barton had shouted almost before what he had seen had registered properly. One of the stacks of heavy crates teetered for a moment and then began to fall towards where Snowey was crouching.

From his position, Snowey looked up, startled. The mass was moving towards him. The crates were falling slowly, slowly. It seemed an age as they came down towards him.

Horrified, Barton watched the heavy wooden crates smash into the floor at almost the exact spot Snowey had been crouching. Then, from the top of the next pile of crates, Dick Barton saw a dark shape in a flat cap. The crates moved as the figure leapt on to the next stack. Dick Barton took a flying leap after the figure, and grabbing hold of the top of the nearest pile, managed to heave himself up on to it. After standing for a few seconds to get his bearing, Barton chased the fleeing figure across the warehouse, leaping from one pile of crates to another. Whoever it was was obviously heading for the window at the far end of the building. Dick Barton saw a chance to cut him off and took it.

He caught up with the mystery man as he was struggling with the window. But Barton was in luck, the window was jammed. The thug turned as he sensed someone behind him, and reached into the inside pocket of his jacket for a gun.

Barton tried one of his famous rugby tackles, and brought the man to the floor. As he fell, his cloth cap came off revealing a head that was completely hairless. Then, a heavy boot landed in Barton's face, and he was forced to let go.

As he got to his feet he was in time to see the window shattering as his adversary dived straight through it.

It was only seconds later that Barton himself arrived at the opening. The cold night air blasted in. The ground outside was littered with broken wood and shards of glass. And, crunching over the debris, he could hear the sound of feet. Leaning out further he saw a large lorry waiting with its engine running, and the bald headed man was wrenching open the door of the passenger seat. Seconds later, the lorry roared away towards the warehouse gates.

Meantime, Snowey White had managed to scramble out from the pile of crates. Luckily, they had only given him a glancing blow. As he looked up, he saw Dick Barton coming towards him over the top of a pile of crates.

'Blighter got away, I'm afraid. You all right, Snowey?'

Rubbing his head ruefully, Snowey said: 'Not so dusty, sir. The old onion's taking a beating tonight, but I missed the worst of it, thanks to you.'

Barton vaulted lightly down from the crates. 'Well, at least we know who one of our adversaries is now.'

Snowey got to his feet. 'You know him, sir?'

'Indeed I do, Snowey – Curly Cohen – a very ugly customer in every sense of the word.'

Snowey was slightly disappointed. 'That's it, then, sir, is it?'

'Hardly, Snowey,' Barton said firmly. 'Curly's strictly small time. A former pugilist who hangs around the East End picking up what crumbs of dirty work he can from the big boys.'

Snowey didn't quite understand all this. But he was beginning to enjoy being back in action again – in spite of his sore 'onion'. 'Still . . . '

'Just before that bit of excitement you said you'd seen something.'

'That's right! I did see something – it must be down there under them crates now.' He pointed to where they had fallen. 'Something sparkling.'

'Well,' Barton replied, as he rubbed his hands together and started to walk towards the pile. 'Let's get to it.'

Barton began to push at the top crate. But the thing was heavier than he had expected. 'Give us a hand, Snowey. Put those well known muscles to use.'

Snowey walked over to the pile. 'Right you are, sir. I could do with a bit of exercise.'

Together, they both began to heave and push at the crate. It was Snowey's help that did the trick. After a moment, the crate began to slide. A bit more effort, and down it went, unblocking the aisle.

Snowey spotted what he was after. 'There! There it is, sir.'

He pointed towards the glistening thing that lay on the floor in a space between two crates.

Dick Barton squeezed into the small space, and bent down and picked it up. It turned out to be something that he recognised. He held it up and said thoughtfully: 'One of Miss Marley's, I think.'

35

'It's an ear-ring, sir.'

'That's right, Snowey. And there's something else, too.'

When he had finished speaking, Dick Barton bent down again and squeezed into the small space. When he emerged he was clutching two tiny scraps of torn newspaper.

'These look as if they've been deliberately torn from whatever paper it was.'

Snowey watched as Barton examined the newspaper. He was impatient. 'What do they say?'

Barton looked at his companion. 'Just the two words,' he said slowly. 'One's got the word "chase" on it; the other word is "ever".'

Snowey scratched his head in bewilderment. 'Chase ever?'

'Or ever chase,' Barton muttered.

'Neither way don't seem to mean a lot,' Snowey commented after a while.

'No,' Barton agreed. He was thinking hard. 'But Miss Marley obviously meant them to mean something and equally obviously meant us to find them.'

They looked at each other in puzzlement. The mystery was getting deeper.

Later that same night, outside the peeling logo that read 'W. H. Brattigan and Sons', Barton and Snowey were sitting in the Riley Monaco. They were having trouble. The starter motor was turning but the engine wouldn't catch.

Barton frowned at his predicament. It was highly unusual for the Riley to break down on him. It was a piece of quality machinery and he took care to see that it was maintained in impeccable condition. He pressed the starter button again The same thing happened.

'Strange,' Dick Barton muttered. Then, he looked across to Snowey, who nodded at him, and they got out of the car from their respective sides.

It was a cold night for mechanics, and Barton suspected that whatever had happened was nothing to do with a lack of maintenance. He lifted the bonnet.

'Look at that sir,' Snowey said almost immediately.

And there, to the side of the well designed engine that had made the name of Riley famous in the racing fraternity, was a carburettor that had been deliberately smashed.

36

'Someone's deliberately sabotaged us, Snowey.' It made Barton furious to see such craftsmanship so crudely damaged.

'Carburettor looks like it's been through the mangle,' Snowey commented sympathetically. He knew how the governor felt about his car.

'I noticed an all-night garage up the road,' Dick Barton said. 'We'll get a cab home.'

They started to walk down the street.

It was about a quarter of an hour later when Barton spotted a cab with its sign lit up.

'Taxi!'

The cab stopped, pulled into the side of the road, and the driver leaned out. 'Where to, gents?'

'Somerset Mansions,' Barton said as he walked across and began to open the door. 'But first stop at the all night garage up the road.'

'Right you are,' the cabbie replied. Then after Snowey and Barton had got in, he changed gear and set off.

The garage was the usual kind of place that stayed open all hours in the East End. There were a few petrol pumps, a small kiosk, and behind these, a few large sheds that must, Barton thought, be the workshops. The taxi drew into the forecourt.

'Just tell them where the car is, Snowey,' Barton said as his ex-sergeant got out of the car. 'And that it'll need a new carburettor.'

'Right Mr Barton,' Snowey made his way towards the garage.

It was then that the cabbie turned around in his seat. 'Not Mr Dick Barton is it, guv?'

'That's what my identity card says.'

'Lumme,' said the cabbie, with a look of astonishment on his face. 'This is a turn-up for the book and no error. There's a china of mine awaiting for you at your flat.'

A smile crossed Dick Barton's face.

The man waiting for them was huddled in the doorway of Somerset Mansions with a cocoon of overcoats over him. He was obviously a determined character, Barton thought, as he got out his door key. And an enthusiastic one too.

37

Barton had scarcely introduced himself when the cabbie started to talk furiously

'I sees you drive up and the young lady get out, then – just as you was driving away – these two men – nasty looking characters – comes up to her.'

Barton let himself into the hall. Snowey and the cabbie followed behind.

'Then what?'

'I'm telling you, ain't I?' The cabbie continued. 'They comes up to her – she was looking for the key in her bag – and they says something to her. Course – I couldn't hear what they said – not at that distance.'

'Quite.'

The cabbie readjusted his pile of overcoats, then rubbed his hands together. 'But anyway, whatever it was they said, they said it and she goes off with them in the lorry.'

A look of interest had crossed Barton's face at the cabbie's last words. 'A Leyland registration number,' he said shrewdly.

'Right!' The cabbie was amazed at Barton's piece of deduction.

The special agent turned to Snowey. 'The same lorry our friend Curly got away in tonight.'

'I'd noticed the number cos it was parked just up the street and I thought to myself, I thought, that's a queer place for a lorry, I thought.' The cabbie was becoming quite competitive.

Barton wanted to get to the bottom of the matter. 'Did she resist them at all?'

'Nah! Went off quiet as you please, guv.'

Snowey didn't like the sound of that: 'That's queer, Mr Barton, isn't it?'

'Not at all, Snowey.' Barton had already been making a series of fast connections. 'Not if they told her they were taking her to her brother.'

The penny dropped with Snowey. 'Oh,' he commented.

Barton took out his pigskin wallet and turned towards the cabbie who was still engaged in burrowing himself into his overcoats. 'Well chum,' he said as he extracted two crisp one pound notes. 'You seem to have earned your two quid.'

The cabbie took the money without protesting. He hadn't been hanging about all night for nothing. 'Thanks squire, you're a gent.'

Then the cabbie left and Dick Barton went into the living room of his flat followed by Snowey who was yawning something terrible. But, still as crisp as ever, Barton strode over to the telephone and dialled a number.

As he watched Barton wait to be connected, Snowey began to wonder, and not for the first time, where the governor got his energy from. He still seemed fresh as the proverbial daisy and they'd already been on the go more than half the night.

'Scotland Yard?' Barton was saying into the telephone. 'Detective Inspector Harrington, please . . . Hello, Jimmy . . . Dick Barton . . . I want you to do me a favour . . . Oh – that was nothing.'

Snowey had an idea of what was going on now. He knew that Dick Barton had helped the police in the past. He tried to stifle another yawn as the telephone conversation continued.

'Wouldn't you have done the same . . . ? Right then. No – I've run across a spot of skulduggery and I want to trace the owners of a lorry that seems to be mixed up in it.'

Snowey then heard Barton give the registration number of the Leyland vehicle that they had seen at the warehouse in Barking.

'What?' There was surprise in Barton's voice. 'That's right. Where? Right – we'll meet you there '

Barton put the phone down and turned towards Snowey. 'Here we go again then,' he said.

Snowey heaved himself up from the armchair he had just settled into. A grin crossed his tired face. He followed his governor out.

Then, when they were sitting in a taxi speeding across London once more, Barton began to explain.

'It appears that the very same lorry was involved in a robbery at a bonded warehouse earlier tonight.' He glanced at his watch. 'Or should I say this morning?'

Snowey didn't even try to stifle his yawns anymore. 'Call

it what you blooming well like, sir; it's past my bed-time, I know that.'

The bonded warehouse was a very different affair from the premises that they had visited in Barking earlier that same night. It was quite an impressive building with a stucco covered front, wrought iron railings, and a pair of high iron gates leading into the loading yard.

The taxi dropped Barton and Snowey outside, a police constable opened the gates for them, and there were other signs of official activity; two police cars and an ambulance were parked nearby, and around the immense sliding doors of the warehouse, a group of fingerprint experts were working

Dick Barton strode across the yard to where a burly character was standing in conversation with two colleagues. Barton had no difficulty in recognising Detective Inspector Harrington – they'd met on several occasions in the past, and had developed a respect for each other. More particularly, Harrington had developed a respect for the Barton powers of deduction.

'This is a rum 'un, Mr Barton,' Harrington remarked when Barton appeared by his side.

'Why so rum, Jimmy?'

Harrington seemed glad to have someone to talk to about the mysterious occurrence. 'They go to all the trouble to break in here, cosh the watchman and tie him up, then don't do anything.'

'Nothing?'

'Not a blessed thing,' Harrington continued. A look of bewilderment crossed his face. 'I'm flummoxed, I don't mind telling you.'

'Doesn't make much sense, does it?' Dick Barton was also puzzled.

'It doesn't make any sense at all.' It was apparent to Dick Barton that Harrington's notions of thievery were confounded. 'They had all the time in the world and they didn't take a thing.'

'What's in this warehouse?' Barton said to Harrington as Snowey appeared at his side after finishing his look around.

'Tobacco.'

40

'How much?'

'About half a million quid's worth,' Harrington replied slowly.

Snowey let out a quiet whistle.

'Right,' Harrington commented. 'That lorry, they could have got away with a dozen bales, I reckon?'

'Worth?' Barton wanted as much information as he could obtain.

Harrington shrugged his shoulders. 'Fifty thou'.'

'And they just didn't bother?' There was a thoughtful expression on Barton's face.

Harrington seemed happier now that he was back in the world of routine officialdom. 'We've checked against the bills of loading. Not one bale missing – not one.'

Even Snowey began to wonder how the governor was going to get to the bottom of this one.

'How do you know this lorry was involved?' Barton asked.

Still dealing with facts already known, Harrington was confident once again. 'That's how the whole thing was discovered,' he said. 'One of our men on the beat saw it coming out of the gates an hour or so ago – thought it was suspicious and came in to investigate.'

'Suspicious it certainly is,' Barton commented to himself. Then to the Detective Inspector: 'Thanks, Jimmy.'

'Any time, Mr Barton,' Harrington replied.

Dick Barton turned away and began to walk back towards the gate. Snowey followed him.

Harrington called after him: 'How are you involved in all this Mr Barton?'

The special agent turned, he had a smile on his face. 'I'll keep you informed, as they say.'

Harrington grinned back. 'You're a close one, you are.'

And all Snowey wanted to do was to go to bed.

It was the next day by the time Dick Barton and Snowey arrived at the East End garage where they had left the Riley Monaco the night before. Frankly, Barton didn't hold out much hope that it would be ready, like everything else on the car, the carburettor was a delicate piece of workmanship, and skill was needed to repair it.

He walked over to the front of the workshop where the car was parked. A mechanic was standing over the open bonnet. He was small and wiry with sandy hair and a moustache. He was somewhere in his mid twenties.

'How's it going?' Barton asked.

'Och, just about finished,' answered the mechanic. He had a Glaswegian accent.

'That's pretty good going,' Barton commented.

The mechanic looked up. 'Well – you know – it's good to get your hands on a decent piece of machinery for a change.'

The man was obviously a craftsman, Barton thought. 'You enjoy your work?'

'Och yes,' the Scot replied. 'I just love machines. I was an apprentice at Derby before the war.'

'Derby?'

'Rolls-Royce,' the mechanic said proudly. 'That's why they put me in REME for the war – taking tanks apart and putting them together again.' He gestured towards the car. 'I'll give it a go now.'

He straightened up from bending over the engine, and went round to the driver's door. Then, he reached inside, switched on the ignition and pressed the starter button. Quickly, the engine fired and began to run smoothly. However, the mechanic didn't seem quite satisfied. He listened for a moment, and after reaching for a screw-driver, went around to the bonnet once more, and started to adjust the carburettor.

'There,' he commented when he was finished. 'I couldn't get a new carburettor for you, of course, but I've bodged up the old one – it'll keep you moving for a few thousand miles while I get the spare.'

Barton was impressed. He always liked to see a skilled man at work. 'You're a pretty dab hand with a screw-driver, that's obvious. What's your name?'

'John Anderson,' said the Scotsman. 'People call me Jock.' He broke into a smile.

What is the meaning of the tobacco robbery that never was? Who is the man so desperate to attain his ends that he will attempt to kill for them?

Will Dick Barton succeed in finding Virginia Marley and her brother, Rex?

Read the next chapter of: Dick Barton – Special Agent.

Chapter Four

Rex Marley, crooner in the grip of drug addiction, and his sister Virginia have both been abducted. In his search for them Dick Barton finds the trail growing increasingly complex. An attempt is made on his life – and there is an apparently meaningless burglary from a warehouse from which nothing is stolen . . .

Now read on.

It was early afternoon, once more Dick Barton found himself sitting in an easy chair in the study of Sir Richard Marley's home. He was feeling relaxed, but alert, and ready for further trouble. He was reporting to Sir Richard on the progress so far. Snowey stood silently behind him. Sir Richard was still agitated, he was pacing up and down in front of them.

'It doesn't make sense, Dick,' Sir Richard said – and not for the first time.

'It makes sense all right,' Barton contradicted the peer. 'It's just that we can't see it yet.'

Sir Richard appeared to be unconvinced. He continued his pacing. 'But what has the warehouse robbery got to do with Virginia?' His tone was one of exasperation.

Coolly, Dick Barton elaborated on the position. 'The self same lorry that she was taken away in was used by the people who broke into the warehouse and who tried to eliminate Snowey and me.'

'I don't like this, Dick, I don't mind telling you.'

Barton grinned wryly at his former employer. 'None too

43

keen on it myself, as a matter of fact, sir.' Then he reached into his pocket. 'We did find one clue, however – at least it may be a clue.' When he had finished speaking, he handed the diamond ear-ring that he had found in the warehouse in Barking over to Sir Richard.

'This is Virginia's!' exclaimed the peer.

Barton's reply was crisp: 'My thought exactly.'

'It belonged to her mother.' Sir Richard's voice had a wistful quality.

'We found it at the warehouse,' Barton explained further. 'Together with these scraps of paper.'

Sir Richard eagerly took the torn fragments and examined them closely.

'Each seems to have been torn out with the purpose of drawing attention to one particular word,' Dick Barton said as Sir Richard looked at the fragments.

'Yes, I see that. "Chase" and "ever".'

'Does it mean anything to you?' the special agent asked.

Sir Richard looked at the torn scraps, then shook his head in puzzlement. ' "Chase"? "Ever"? Nothing. No! Wait a minute!' He paused to think. 'Of course – what a fool I am! Taken together with the ear-ring – Ever Ring Chase.'

Barton didn't understand. 'Ever Ring Chase?'

'It's the name of a house near my own place in the country. Been empty now for years.'

Barton looked up at Snowey, but ex-Sergeant White didn't need telling. He was already making his way towards the door.

Ever Ring Chase was a decaying Victorian Country mansion in the Gothic style. There were turrets covered in lead sheeting that was now going green with neglect, porticos and balustrades in a bad state of repair. Plaster was peeling from the front of the house showing ugly scars in the brickwork. The house itself had a brooding, sinister atmosphere, that was echoed by the overgrown gardens. Laurels and rhododendrons were spreading over each side of the drive. Further back, there was a tangle of undergrowth and some taller trees that had once formed a well kept spinney.

44

Dick Barton stopped his car just inside the sagging gates that hung from two stone columns. He got out and stood for a moment, looking at the house. Snowey emerged from the other side of the car.

'Not exactly Homes and Gardens is it, Snowey?'

'More like Ghoulies and Ghosties,' came the reply.

'Shanks's pony from here, I think,' Barton suggested, as he moved cautiously into the undergrowth that flanked the drive. Snowey followed carefully.

They threaded their way through the dense mass of greenery, and made for the general direction of the house. The atmosphere was close and heavy. Dick Barton had a sense of foreboding, that somewhere in this evil environment, someone was up to no good. He hoped Virginia and Rex were safe.

Suddenly, from somewhere behind them, a twig snapped. They both stopped dead. Expectancy filled the air.

'What was that?' Snowey whispered.

Barton shook his head. Slowly, he turned to stare behind him. Snowey also looked in that direction. But there was nothing definite, only a tension that somehow seemed to come out of the environment itself. Snowey nervously licked his lips.

'One of them wild animals, I expect,' he said.

'Such as what?' asked Barton sceptically.

'Lumme, guv, I dunno,' came the reply. 'Whatever they go in for in this blooming jungle.' He breathed heavily. 'Give me the streets of dear old London any day of the week. You know where you are with pavements.'

'Well,' Barton said seriously. 'Whatever it was it seems to have gone to earth now. Let's get a move on.'

Snowey was about to obey Dick Barton's instruction when there was a vicious whir just above his head. A thump followed almost immediately. When he looked up he saw an arrow buried in an oak tree. It had missed the governor's head by inches.

'Quick, Snowey – get down!'

They hurled themselves to the ground.

'The natives appear to be hostile,' Dick Barton said as he lay on the ground.

'Too blooming right sir,' Snowey agreed. 'Downright unfriendly, if you was to ask me.'

They waited for a moment. Then, Barton scanned the trees around them for evidence of any further movement. The undergrowth was so thick that he couldn't see very far. Still, he was sure that if there was anything there, he would have spotted it. Satisfied, he got cautiously to his feet, and tugged at the arrow that was deeply embedded in the tree. After a moment, it came free. He looked closely at the arrow head.

'What's more, they mean business,' he said to Snowey. 'Take a sniff of that.'

Barton held the arrow out towards Snowey, who took a step forward and was about to grasp it.

'No! Don't touch it.'

Snowey leant forward and sniffed at the point. 'Phew! Smells as if something died and forgot to get itself buried.'

'Curare,' Barton said knowingly.

'That poison stuff?'

'Got it in one,' Barton commented. He added warningly; 'One scratch from that and you're a goner.'

'Yeah – ' Snowey said. 'I read about that stuff in the *Sunday Pic*. Paralyses you, don't it?'

Carefully, Barton deposited the arrow in the ground. 'That's right. We're dealing with a toxicological toxopholite.'

'Oh – yes,' Snowey grinned. 'We had one of those but the wheels come off.'

But the moment of humour didn't last long. Suddenly, a terrible cry came from behind them. They whirled around to see a grotesque and frightening figure. An apparition of evil dressed in a full set of fifteenth century Japanese armour, with a grimacing mask on top. The figure was seated on a galloping horse and carrying a naked Samurai sword. A bow was slung on his back.

'Wait for it, Snowey,' Barton said coolly.

The moments ticked by. An eternity passed right there on the track as Barton and Snowey waited for the galloping figure to come nearer. And nearer.

When the horseman was only ten yards away Barton shouted his command: 'Scatter!'

They moved in opposite directions leaving the horseman only an empty space to ride through. Snowey felt the rush of air as the Samurai sword whished by his ear. And then, as suddenly as it had come, the figure was gone. From what seemed far away, they heard him crashing into the undergrowth.

'Phew!' Snowey said as they regrouped.

'Couldn't have put it better myself,' Barton said as he pushed his hair back into place. 'Come on.'

They only stopped again when they came to the edge of the spinney. It was on a slightly higher level than the house, which was down in a dip. From where they were standing, they could see the remnants of what had once been the front lawn. Wanting to stay in cover, they turned back into the spinney once more.

They found their way at an angle from which they could not be seen from the house. Barton led the way as they sprinted across the yard which fronted the stable block at the back of the house. He stopped at the corner, looked around, and seeing nothing, he jerked his head for Snowey to follow.

Cautiously, they made their way towards the back of the house.

'Look, Mr Barton,' Snowey said. He pointed to a set of tyre marks on the ground in front of them. 'There's been a lorry up here recently.'

'You're right,' Barton replied. 'Good work, Snowey.'

Following the direction of the tyre marks, they turned a corner and found themselves facing a different part of the large stables. A lorry that Barton recognised was parked outside.

'The old familiar meat wagon again,' Barton commented.

They crossed over to the Leyland, but found no one inside the cab. Snowey then went around the back of the lorry. The door was open but there was nothing inside. He reported back to Barton.

'Let's have a look in here,' Barton said. He opened the large door that led into the stable itself.

The stables had once been whitewashed, but now there were only a few flakes still clinging to the walls. There was a cobbled floor with a channel for drainage, and along the far wall, wooden compartments divided the place up into about twenty stalls.

Barton stood in the doorway for a second or two. Then, satisfied that there was no one around, he crossed to one of the stalls and peered over the rail.

Snowey heard the governor let out a long, low whistle. He walked across to join him. Inside the stall, he could see two large bales covered with sacking.

'What's that, sir, do you reckon?'

'I'm not sure, Snowey – but I've got a darned good idea.' When he had finished speaking, Dick Barton opened the door to the stall and went in. Then turning to Snowey, he said: 'Got your knife, Snowey?'

From his pocket, Snowey produced the large clasp knife that he always carried. It had seen him through the War. Once, he'd nearly lost it on the beach in Normandy, and had to knock out a Jerry machine gun nest before he got it back. He was fond of it. He handed it to Dick Barton.

Barton took the knife, opened the blade, and, with one upward sweep of his arm, slit through the sacking. 'Yes,' he said to himself after he had examined the contents.

'Horse food?' Snowey asked.

'No,' came Barton's crisp reply. 'Tobacco.'

'Tobacco,' Snowey echoed. 'You mean – ?'

'Yes.' Barton stood up. 'That's exactly what I mean – from the warehouse robbery.'

'But they said nothing was missing.' Snowey had a bewildered expression on his face.

'Bit of a conundrum, isn't it?' Barton came out of the stall, and peered over the rail into the next one.

'And more.'

He looked into the one next to that.

'And more.'

Snowey stood there watching as Dick Barton went down the whole length of the building looking into each stall as he went. When he'd finished, Barton turned around and began to walk back slowly.

'Twenty in all,' Dick Barton announced. 'Now just what is our friend up to, Snowey?'

'Maybe he's a heavy smoker, sir.'

48

'Maybe.' Barton smiled back. Then he stopped talking, and held up his hand to indicate that they should be quiet. 'What's that?' he asked softly.

From some way away, they heard the sound of voices.

Still keeping his voice low, Dick Barton made a suggestion: 'Let's have a dekko, eh?'

They went out of the stables, quickly across the yard, and disappeared into the undergrowth once more.

Barton and Snowey could see the front of the house from the vantage point they had chosen in the shrubbery. There was a large Rolls-Royce parked at the bottom of the steps which led up to the house. Dick Barton recognised the model. It was a 20/25 of 1934 vintage. A fine car. But the action that was going on around it was of a different quality altogether.

An elegantly dressed man was watching as a woman, and a man in a chauffeur's uniform, whom Barton recognised as Curly Cohen, were supporting a semi-comatose figure as they descended the steps. Barton also recognised the figure they were helping – if that was the right word. It was none other than the missing crooner and drug addict – Rex Marley.

Rex didn't look in too good a shape, Barton thought. He was unshaven and his hands were tied behind his back.

The elegantly dressed man spoke: 'Get Mr Marley into the Rolls.'

'Righto, Mr Hetherington,' Curly Cohen replied.

The man called Hetherington broke into an angry retort: 'Don't use my name! I've told you a hundred times.'

Hidden in the shrubbery, Barton and Snowey exchanged glances. It was very clear that some dirty business was going on.

'If we was to jump them now, sir,' Snowey suggested in a whisper.

Dick Barton shook his head. 'We still don't know where Virginia is.'

There was a slight pause before Snowey spoke again. 'Who's this Hetherington bloke?'

'I don't know,' Barton replied. 'The name seems familiar.'

They turned their attention to the front of the house again. Now Curly and the woman were busy bundling Rex Marley into the back of the Rolls, and Hetherington was standing nearby, issuing more instructions.

'Curly – you take Marley to the other place. Melissa and I will bring his sister in the lorry.'

'Righto, guv,' the thug in chauffeur's uniform replied.

Barton and Snowey were still watching as Curly Cohen slid into the driving seat of the car.

'Snowey,' Barton ordered. 'Get down to the car and follow the Rolls. I'm going back to the lorry to await developments.'

And with that, the special agent and his aide de camp edged back into the undergrowth. Snowey glanced back as they went. He saw Curly Cohen start the engine, and Hetherington and Melissa, whom he was pretty sure was the girl with the gun in her muff, go back up the steps to the house.

From this point, the team split up. Snowey hurried back through the spinney towards Barton's Riley.

Meantime, Barton himself had arrived in the front of the stables where the lorry was parked.

And, in a room in the house that had once been elegant, but was now empty of furniture and crumbling with neglect, the progress of the special agent was being watched.

Hetherington turned away from the window. 'It's working, Mr Melganik,' he said.

The man called Melganik was sitting in the only chair in the room. He was about fifty five years old, with a bearing that would have been elegant except for the hideous vertical scar that ran down from his eyebrows to his chin. When he spoke it was with a voice that Sir Richard Marley, had he been present, would have recognised.

'Of course it's working,' Melganik said in his sibilant, mid European tones. 'I'm afraid that brain power is not our friend Barton's strong point.'

There was a stirring from behind the master criminal. Of the two women present, one was lying on the floor, bound and gagged. Her eyes smouldered with rage at Melganik's remark about Dick Barton. She was loyal to her

50

father's friend. Her name was Virginia Marley.

Melissa, who had been standing near Melganik, glanced down in contemptuous fashion at Virginia.

'I think our little kitten is fearful for Mr Barton's safety,' she said derisively.

The master criminal chuckled in the sparsely furnished room. 'And well she might be, Melissa. And well she might be.'

Virginia Marley struggled helplessly against the ropes that bound her.

Snowey White hurried towards Dick Barton's Riley which was still parked in front of the sagging front gates of Ever Ring Chase. When he reached the car, he flung open the driver's door, got in and started the engine, then put it in gear and reversed into the undergrowth of the spinney that threatened to engulf the drive.

Once he was sure that the car was well hidden, Snowey switched off the engine, and peered through the windscreen to await developments.

He didn't have to wait long. Within minutes, the 1934 Rolls Royce 20/25, with Curly Cohen at the wheel, began to glide past.

Snowey waited until he was sure that the Rolls was going past him. He peered through the windscreen again, and saw the car go through the gates and on to the country road.

Snowey held his breath and counted ten. Then, he started the engine again, put his foot down on the accelerator, and the Riley burst out of the undergrowth in pursuit of the Rolls.

By this time, Dick Barton had reached the lorry that Hetherington had been talking about. He walked around the back, and went into the interior through the open rear door. There was no sign of Virginia, yet he was sure that Hetherington had said she was going to be taken there.

He looked around the inside. It struck him immediately that this was not the usual sort of goods vehicle. The thick, insulated sides indicated that it was probably a refrigerated truck, used for transporting meat.

51

There were footsteps from outside. Quickly, he made for the only place in which he could hide; in the corner behind the doors. He pressed himself as far into the corner as possible. At the very least, he could not be seen from outside.

But unexpectedly, no one came into the lorry. He heard the sound of footsteps on gravel. They stopped, and then, the heavy doors began to swing shut, and he heard the bolts being slid home. He walked to the door and examined it. There was no way that he could get out.

The Rolls was still in front of Snowey, and he drove carefully, taking care to keep a good distance between them. He saw the driver crane around, but he was sure that he could not be spotted.

But, inside the Rolls, Curly Cohen was chuckling to himself. 'Sucker,' he said softly. He continued to drive on.

If Dick Barton could have seen Hetherington climb into the driver's seat, and the self satisfied smirk on Melganik the master criminal's face as the former carried out his orders, then undoubtedly he would have been even more concerned than he was.

'A trap,' he muttered to himself, as he made a thorough search of the interior of the refrigeration lorry.

There were no weak spots in the entire structure. The floor and walls were made of metal, and the only real feature of the whole interior was a small grille in the middle of the ceiling.

While Dick Barton was still searching, the grille suddenly crackled into life. Melganik's silky tones came through the static: 'Hello, Mr Barton. We have not had the pleasure, I think of conversing before.'

Dick Barton had no intention of letting them see what a fix he was in. His voice had a jaunty quality when he spoke. 'The pleasure is entirely yours, Mr . . . ?'

'Names scarcely matter at this juncture,' continued the voice. 'You see, as you will have gathered, this is a refrigeration truck . . . '

Barton heard the voice pause.

'In a moment you will hear the gentle hum of the refrigeration unit going into action . . . so . . . '

Melganik was speaking into a microphone from the cab at the front of the lorry. He depressed a switch.

Inside the body of the truck, Dick Barton heard the gentle hum as the refrigeration unit started up. He looked up the grille. 'Looks like we're in for a cold snap,' he commented.

The reply began in a chuckle. 'Snap – how very appropriate. You see, Mr Barton, this truck is now going to be concealed in a remote part of the grounds. No one can possibly find you. The refrigeration unit will continue to function for at least twenty four hours – until its fuel runs out. But by that time you will be a solid block of ice, Mr Barton. I do so hope that those who eventually find you will not "snap" you in two when they come to lift you out.'

Through the speaker that was fitted into the cabin of the lorry as part of the two way communication system, Melganik heard Barton's reply: 'Why not? Then there'll be two Dick Bartons to stop your filthy business instead of one.'

'Two?' Melganik said angrily into the microphone. 'I could deal with a dozen!' Then, he switched off the microphone and handed it back to Hetherington who was sitting at the wheel beside him.

Melganik got out of the cab and joined Melissa, the lady who specialised in automatic pistols. He waved Hetherington on. 'Go,' he shouted.

From Snowey White's point of view there wasn't much action at all. He was still driving after the Rolls, still keeping his distance, and still wondering what the governor was up to back at Ever Ring Chase. He turned a bend in the road, and slowed the Riley.

There was a fork up ahead. He brought the Riley to a stop. He didn't know what to make of it. The major road, the one he was now on, stretched ahead for a good half mile. There was no traffic on it at all.

The other road was narrow and winding, he reckoned that it was the more likely choice, so heaved the wheel over hard and went on down.

In a field at the side of the road, concealed by the hedge,

Curly Cohen sat grinning with satisfaction. Making sure that Snowey was out of sight, he started the engine of the Rolls, and headed back down the major road again.

Hetherington sat in the driver's seat of the refrigeration truck as it bumped its way over the rough ground. He chose his way carefully, steering between trees until the lorry was lost out of sight in the wood.

Then, when he was sure that the whole vehicle could not be seen from any angle, Hetherington stopped and cut the engine. He got out of the cab, checked once more. Then he fastidiously dusted off his hands and clothes and headed back in the general direction of the house.

Dick Barton felt the lorry come to a stop. He was glad when it did, trying to cling to its sides as it went over the bumpy ground wasn't exactly his idea of a picnic. He heard the engine die away, and then there was nothing. Only a sinister silence, and already, a sense of creeping cold.

He listened intently for any sound of action from outside. There was nothing. Not even the sibilant tones of the sinister arch criminal. Not even a bird.

'Hello!'

He beat against the sides of the lorry in an attempt to attract attention.

'Hello.'

There was no response. Dick Barton's breath was beginning to condense on the air in front of his face. He shivered and began to slap his arms around his body in an attempt to keep his circulation going.

Already, crusts of ice were beginning to form at the top of the vehicle. He could feel the ends of his fingers going numb. There was no point in wasting energy. It was too cold. Much too cold.

Is this the end for Barton, left to a hideous, lingering death by the sinister Melganik and his henchmen?
Read the next chapter of: Dick Barton – Special Agent.

Chapter Five

*Dick Barton, hot on the trail of the abducted crooner Rex
Marley and his sister Virginia, is trapped in a refrigerated
lorry with Snowey sent off on a wild goose chase by the
master criminal Melganik.*
   Now read on.

Each breath was now like drawing in icicles. Dick Barton
watched as the ice forming on the sides of the refrigerated truck which was well concealed in the woods surrounding Ever Ring Chase, crept down further and
further.
   In desperation, he began to beat on the sides of the
lorry with his fists again.
   He stopped. Then, he began to blow on his hands in an
attempt to warm them.

The road was getting narrower and narrower. Snowey
White was wondering what to do as the hedge loomed
over the sides of the Riley Monaco, and threatened to
meet overhead.
   He had to slow the car anyway. He couldn't get up any
speed at all. The road was getting worse; it was petering
off into a rough track.
   He decided that he'd better stop the car altogether. It
was useless going any further. He put his foot on the
brakes. They couldn't have got a Rolls through. They
must have given him the slip back there where the main
road forked.

Cold threatened to engulf him. He began to stamp up
and down in the confined space in an effort to keep his
circulation going. Then, when Dick Barton started to slap

55

his arms around his body again, he noticed a bulge in his jacket pocket. He stopped and felt for the object. It was Snowey's clasp knife. He must have forgotten to give it back to him. Still, it looked as if it might come in useful now.

He unfolded the blade and walked across to the metal wall. He tried to dig it into the metal, but met with no success. Then, he had an idea. He looked again at the knife, and unfolded the other side – a long, pointed instrument that was intended for removing stones from horses' hooves.

This time he might be more successful.

Snowey decided to turn back. He reversed Barton's car in a nearby gateway, and put his foot down on the accelerator. He was going back the way he had come. He had a feeling that there was a lot of catching up to do.

Dick Barton stood at the front end of the lorry. The pointed end of the clasp knife was open. He held that in his left hand and was using it as a punch in an attempt to make an opening. In his right hand, he held his shoe. He was using it as a hammer. The exertion was helping to keep him warm. And, with luck it might even help him to escape.

Snowey drove through the gates of Ever Ring Chase, and steered off the drive into the cover of the spinney. After making sure that it was well concealed, he began to walk cautiously towards the house. He didn't want to meet any poison arrows or sinister gentleman with Samurai swords this time.

Dick Barton had managed to make a small hole in the front wall of the lorry. After opening the blade of the clasp knife once more, he had twisted it around to enlarge the hole. Satisfied, he turned his attention to the thin strips of metal beading that covered the joints in the metal sheets that formed the wall. Using the knife as a screwdriver this time, he started to unscrew one of the six screws that held the beading in place.

By this time, Snowey had reached the stable yard. But there was nothing around. Not even a dickey bird, or more particularly there was no sign of a Leyland lorry whose registration number had been noted by Dick Barton and which had taken part in the mysterious tobacco robbery the night before.

For a moment, Snowey stood there puzzled. Then, he made a decision. He started to walk towards the house.

The screws weren't as difficult as he'd expected. He was now working on the last one. But the cold had seeped through to Dick Barton's bones. He was having trouble keeping his hand steady. From time to time, he broke out in a burst of uncontrollable shivering. One of these bouts struck again.

He stopped work and tried to warm his hands under his armpits. He looked at the ice forming on the sides of the refrigeration truck. It had almost reached the floor.

The room which Snowey now entered in Ever Ring Chase was the same one in which Melganik had been sitting sometime previously. But there was now no sign of the master criminal's occupancy. Neither was there any indication that Virginia Marley had been lying, bound and helpless on the floor while Melganik had chuckled, and the special agent had walked into a trap.

He managed the last screw. The piece of beading came away from the wall as he pulled. His hands could hardly manage to touch the bare metal. But Dick Barton had been in situations as difficult as this one before. His four years in the commandos had taught him a lot. And one of the most important things had been ingenuity.

Holding the beading straight, he carried it over to the small hole he had made with the clasp knife, and slowly began to insert the beading into the hole.

Snowey White came out of the decaying Victorian mansion no wiser than when he went in. There was no one about anywhere. All he could see was tyre marks, and a lot of depressing greenery. He was beginning to be concerned about the governor. He cupped his hand around his mouth and began to shout:

'Mr Barton.'

Only silence met his attempt.

'Mr Barton!'

There was no reply. With a frown on his face, Snowey started off down the drive.

There was frost on his hair, and on his clothes and his fingers were blue with cold. But Dick Barton was still working hard. The piece of beading was now threaded right through the hole, and, frowning in concentration, he was gently manipulating it this way and that.

He had an idea. He only hoped he could hold out against the increasing cold until it worked.

He was trying to judge the position of the horn button in the cab at the front of the lorry. If he could get it right, then he could send out the alarm. If . . .

Snowey had reached the sagging gates at the end of the drive. He turned off into the undergrowth, and stood uncertainly near the parked Riley. He didn't like to go off, not until he knew that Dick Barton was all right.

'Mr Barton!'

There was still no reply. Snowey didn't feel happy about going off but couldn't really think what else he could do. He got into the car and slammed the door shut.

Back in the refrigerated lorry, the ice was now creeping across the floor towards Dick Barton. He was still struggling with the strip of metal beading, trying to make contact with the horn in the middle of the steering wheel.

He grinned to himself as he felt it touch the outer rim of the wheel. Gradually, he inched it across. He stopped for a moment, blew on his numb right hand, and then pressed gently.

His reward was one very short blast on the hooter. Then, the beading slipped.

Snowey was about to press the starter button when he heard the sound. He was sure that it was a lorry's horn.

He listened carefully, frowning in concentration. The wind rustled the undergrowth around him. He didn't like this place.

Barton, heavily encrusted with frost, and almost surrounded by the thickening ice, desperately struggled once more with the beading. It was wavering and wavering . . .

Couldn't have been anything, Snowey decided. He shrugged to himself, and pressed the starter button. The engine caught almost immediately. He put the Riley in gear, and edged carefully on to the drive again.

He reached the gates and stopped. There it was again. In the distance. There was no point in mucking about. It must be the governor. He started to run up the drive, back towards the house.

The effort was almost too much for him. He could feel nothing in his hands at all. Numbness was creeping up his arms. He tried to keep the strip of beading in position so that it pressed on the horn but it was increasingly difficult to maintain any pressure.

Dick Barton collapsed to his knees. The combined effect of the freezing cold and effort of working was threatening to prove too much for him. He hoped there was enough pressure on the strip.

Panting, Snowey reached the stable yard. There it was again. He tried to fix the direction of the sound. It was nowhere near the buildings of Ever Ring Chase. It was further away, amongst the trees.

He began to run again. He crossed an open field and made for a dense woodland on the far side. The sound of the lorry horn was growing louder as he ran.

Inside the refrigerated truck, in a temperature many degrees below zero, Dick Barton made his final effort, and then collapsed on the floor. Finally, the special agent was overcome by the cold.

Snowey heard the horn stop, and began to run faster. Then, he paused. He'd lost his direction. He was deep in the woodland now, the trees were casting shadows around him. Then he saw it. It was only just visible – the body of the lorry showed through the trees about twenty yards away. He began to run towards it.

Dick Barton lay slumped against the wall of the truck. Ice was all around him. He was trying to stay awake. He was remembering Virginia as a young girl, and Rex before he had become a drug addict. He knew that if he lost consciousness then that would be the end of him. But he wanted to close his eyes. To drift away into a peaceful place where everything was warm and cosy. He felt his eyes close.

He jolted himself into wakefulness by remembering Rex as he had appeared that night onstage at the Blue Parrot; by thinking about the stricken look of despair that had overtaken Virginia. He must survive.

Suddenly, there was a great crash. The doors were flung open from the outside, and the sunlight streamed in. And standing in the doorway was no one else but Snowey White.

'Mr Barton?'

Dick Barton croaked his reply: 'All present and correct, Snowey.' Then he slumped to the floor.

When he regained consciousness, Dick Barton found himself out in the open air, propped up against a tree. Snowey was standing over him. He was holding a hip flask and pouring some of the contents down Barton's throat. Barton coughed violently as the raw spirit entered his system.

'Jumping Jehosephat, Snowey,' he said weakly. 'Did you make that stuff yourself?'

Snowey grinned back at his ex-captain. He was glad to see him come round. 'It's the last of the schnapps I brought back from Fritzland, sir.' He paused to make sure that Barton was all right. 'I thought you was a goner that time.'

'You were not alone in that supposition,' Barton replied. 'The question is – what now?' Using the tree trunk for support, he tried to struggle to his feet.

'Oughtn't you to rest a bit, sir?'

Dick Barton's answer was decisive. He did not under-estimate the opposition, but he was going to fight them with everything he'd got. 'No time for rest, Snowey. Those swine have still got Miss Marley, remember?'

It was some time later. Barton and Snowey were back once more in the living-room of his flat in Somerset Mansions. Snowey was standing watching as Barton paced impatiently up and down the room. He was glad to see the governor back to his old self, though he didn't know where he got the energy from.

'Hetherington, Hetherington,' Barton was saying to himself as he walked up and down.

'I don't know no one called Hetherington,' Snowey said to no one in particular.

'The name's familiar, that's all,' Barton muttered to himself. I just can't . . . ' he stopped as he tried to concentrate. 'Wait a minute. Snowey – hand me my trusty *Who's Who*.'

Snowey reached up to the nearest shelf, scanned along it quickly, found the volume and handed it down to Barton who leafed through it quickly.

'Hatfield . . . Heslop . . . Hetherington!' Barton's voice rose as he found what he had been looking for. 'Charles, Percy, M.P. Of course! You remember, Snowey!'

Snowey shook his head in reply. He didn't know anything about it.

'Bright young politician before the war,' Dick Barton explained. 'Went to the bad over a woman – forced to resign. Formed his own party – got more and more extreme – fought a few by-elections with no success at all.'

None of it meant much to Snowey. 'I never took much interest in politics,' he said. 'One lot's as bad as the other if you ask me.'

But Dick Barton refused to be drawn into a discussion. He kept his concentration on the glimmer of light at the end of the very murky tunnel. On the character of the renegade M.P. called Hetherington. He turned to Snowey. 'He became very bitter by all accounts.'

61

'I don't see how he comes into all this,' Snowey replied.

'Nor do I, Snowey – yet.' Barton turned towards the door. 'I suggest we pay a little social call on Mr Charles Hetherington, former Member of Parliament.'

Dick Barton and Snowey came out of the doors of Somerset Mansions and stopped dead in their tracks. In the road, an overalled figure was bending over the open bonnet of the Riley Monaco.

'Another piece of sabotage, Snowey,' Dick Barton whispered. 'Go round behind him. I'll try the frontal attack.'

Snowey nodded in reply, and moved quietly off so that he could approach the man from behind and cut off any possibility of retreat.

Barton sauntered casually across to the car, and stood directly behind the overalled figure who was working on the engine with a spanner. Barton waited for a while and then spoke softly: 'I wouldn't try anything if I were you,' he said.

The man looked up startled. He had sandy hair and a thin moustache. He was even more surprised when Snowey grabbed his arms from behind.

'Got him, Sir!'

The sandy haired man was outraged: 'What the heck do you think you're playing at?'

Then, Barton recognised him. 'Oh – it's Jock Anderson, isn't it?'

'I just came round with your new carburettor,' Jock explained. 'Thought I'd fix it for you.'

Dick Barton motioned to Snowey. 'It's okay, Snowey – you remember Jock.'

Snowey released his hold on Jock. 'Oh – sorry mate,' he apologised. 'I thought you was one of the nasties.'

'What business are you two in, anyway?' There was an expression of puzzlement on Jock Anderson's face.

Dick Barton grinned in reply. 'Good question, Jock. We're not quite sure ourselves, yet.' He looked thoughtfully at the mechanic. 'But seeing you gives me an idea. I wonder if you'd do me a favour?'

Snowey grinned now. So the governor was up to his tricks again.

*

The Riley Monaco stopped in the Hampstead Street. After a moment, the driver's door opened, and a very different Dick Barton got out. He was now wearing Jock Anderson's grease stained overalls and a peaked cap. He was carrying a toolbag and looked like what he was supposed to be; an ordinary tradesman on a housecall.

Before he crossed the road to the Hetherington house, Barton turned and spoke to Snowey through the open car window: 'If I'm not out in ten minutes, get in there somehow and create merry hell.'

'We'll find a way, Mr Barton,' came the reply. 'Don't you fret.'

Snowey watched as the special agent disappeared around the corner of the street. Then, he looked at his watch. From the back of the car, came the voice of Jock Anderson.

'He's a cool customer, your Mr Barton,' Jock said in admiration.

'He is that,' Snowey agreed. 'You couldn't wish for a finer officer to serve under.'

Snowey opened the passenger door. 'Come on Jock, my lad. We'd better keep an eye on things.'

In his working clothes, and looking like the tradesman he wasn't, Dick Barton mounted the steps of the bijou Hampstead residence given as the address of Charles Hetherington, former M.P. in his copy of *Who's Who*. He rang the doorbell, and waited. A few moments passed. Then the door was opened by a maid.

'Oui?'

'Beg pardon, miss?' Dick Barton had replaced his cultured tones with a rough working class accent.

'What is it you want?' the maid said.

Dick Barton looked down at the piece of paper he held in his hand. He pretended to consult it. 'Name of Hetherington, wasn't it?' he said after a while.

The reply was sharp: 'Mr Hetherington is out.'

'Ah, well,' Dick Barton said, as he went further into his imitation of the working classes. 'Plumber miss. Taps, wash basin, one – on the blink, savvy?'

The maid looked at him blankly.

'Tap, you know,' he tried again.

There was still no response. Using his ingenuity, Dick Barton mimed a tap being turned out, and made a 'shushing' noise.

She understood now. 'Ah – tap!' She nodded at him eagerly.

'Right,' Barton said. *'Oui! Certainment. Un tap.* Mr Hetherington he telephone, yes? *Telephono?'*

'I do not know this,' the maid replied.

'Well, he telephoned all right,' Barton insisted. 'I can tell you that. Me mend it, right?'

'You had better come in,' she said, as she stood aside.

From the other side of the road, as they sauntered casually past, Snowey White and Jock Anderson saw Dick Barton go into Hetherington's house. The door closed behind him. Snowey nodded at Jock.

In the cellar of the same house, Virginia Marley, who was sitting bound and gagged in a chair, heard the doorbell ring and the front door close. She followed the sound of footsteps on the floor above. Then, she looked at her brother Rex, who was also bound and was lying on an old, stained mattress in the far corner of the dark and damp smelling room.

Curly Cohen, who was standing near the entrance door to the cellar, with a revolver in his hand, sneered as the footsteps passed overhead. 'Your precious Mr Barton, poking his clever nose in again,' he said to Virginia.

The girl glared back at him.

Barton was now standing in the hall of the Hetherington house. The maid was standing in front of him. He pretended to consult his piece of paper again.

'Ground floor, it says,' he announced, as he tried the first door that he came to.

The maid protested. 'No. No. No one must go down there.'

Down below, in the darkened cellar, Curly Cohen stood at the top of the steps as he heard the cellar door being tried. He tensed, and made sure that the safety catch was off

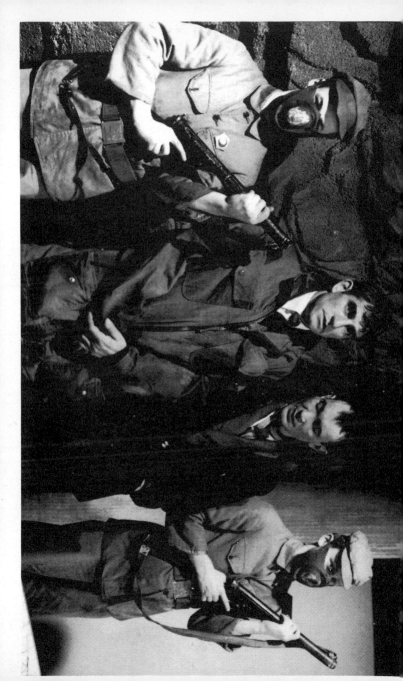

his revolver. Then, as the footsteps receded, he relaxed, and came down the steps.

Virginia watched as the thug looked at his watch, and then went into a small room situated off the main cellar. She took her chance and screamed as loud as she could. The gag was tight on her lips.

Dick Barton was moving away from the cellar door when he heard the muffled scream. He stopped and turned to the maid.

'What was that, Miss?'

She seemed to misunderstand him. 'It is the cellar,' she said.

'No – that noise.'

The maid frowned. 'I heard no noise.'

He decided to play it cool. 'Must have been the mice down there,' he commented. 'If you'll just show me the bathroom.'

The maid then led the way down the hallway.

Curly Cohen had heard Virginia scream. He came running back into the main room of the cellar and slapped the captive woman hard across the face.

'Just keep quiet, that's all,' he said. There was menace in his tone.

Virginia Marley glared at her jailer. It was obvious that the thug had no regard at all for the normal code of decency. She hated him.

Dick Barton was now in the ground floor bathroom fiddling with one of the taps on the washbasin, pretending that there was something wrong with it. Jock Anderson's toolbag was open on the floor beside him. He pretended to sort through his tools.

'I'll need the smaller wrench for this,' he said to the maid who was standing behind him.

'*Comment?*'

'I said, I'll need . . . Oh – never mind. I'll come back later, right?' He began to gather up his tools and replace them in the bag. '*Comprehendez-vous?*'

The maid looked at him blankly

'Ah – never mind.' He picked up the bag and walked out of the ground floor bathroom into the hall, heading for the front door. 'See you later, miss,' he said as he went out.

In the cellar, Curly Cohen nodded to himself with satisfaction as he heard the front door slam. But his attention was soon diverted. There was a buzzing sound from the next room. Curly hurried across the cellar floor, and went into the smaller room which was lit by a single bare electric light bulb. There was a table in the middle of the room, and on the table a radio transmitter. Curly picked up the microphone and began to speak.

'Curly.'

The voice of Melganik, the master criminal, came through the receiver. 'The prying Mr Barton has gone now. For good this time.'

Curly grinned to himself. 'What have you done, Guv?'

'Those fools were stupid enough to leave their car unattended. We have attached a little device, Curly. As soon as the speedometer needle reaches fifty . . . ' the voice broke off into a hideous chuckle.

Eagerly, Curly Cohen asked: 'What? What? What happens?'

The laughing stopped. Then, Melganik spoke with relish: 'The vehicle and its occupants will be blown into a million fragments.'

In the next room, Virginia heard the voice come over the radio. She had no way of warning Dick Barton of the terrible death that awaited him and Snowey. She struggled against the ropes that bound her. She could not escape.

Dick Barton, Snowey and Jock converged on the Riley which was still parked in the Hampstead street. Not a word was spoken until they were inside. No one was going to take a chance of being overheard.

'Well,' Dick Barton said after he'd eased himself in behind the steering wheel. Snowey was by his side, and Jock was in the back, as before. 'We know where they are now.'

'In the house?' Snowey asked.

'Yes,' came the reply. 'The cellar. But the problem is –
how do we get them out?'

There was a pause as both Snowey and Jock considered
the question. Then Snowey spoke suddenly: 'Wait a
minute, sir – look!'

Barton followed the direction in which Snowey was
pointing. Through the side window of the Riley Monaco
he saw a 1934 Rolls Royce 20/25 glide past. And in the
Rolls sat a man whom he recognised immediately.

'Hetherington,' Barton said loudly. He switched on the
ignition and pressed the starter button.

'We going after him, sir?'

'Too right we are, Snowey,' came the reply.

Then, Barton deftly put the Riley into gear and they
began to move off. Barton had to accelerate to keep the
Rolls in sight. The speedometer needle started to flicker
upwards.

Unknown to Dick Barton, Snowey and Jock, that
flickering needle held the key to their future existence.
Once it reached fifty they were doomed. And for their
epitaph they would have only the lingering laugh of the
master criminal Melganik.

'Where the blazes is he going?' Dick Barton was puzzled
by the speed at which Hetherington was travelling.

'He's speeding up again, Mr Barton,' Jock announced.

'Looks like he's heading for the Great North Road,'
Dick Barton said as he kept his eyes on the road ahead.

It was a simple remark. It contained no fear, or aware-
ness that Hetherington, in the Rolls Royce 20/25 was leading them to a horrible death. The speedometer had
reached thirty-five long ago. Now forty was reached, and it
raced suddenly upward towards forty-five . . .

*Is Dick Barton speeding towards death? How has the
former M.P. Hetherington become involved with Melganik and his evil machinations?*

Read the next chapter of: Dick Barton – Special Agent.

Chapter Six

Dick Barton, in a bid to rescue the crooner Rex Marley, and his sister Virginia, gives chase to Charles Hetherington, renegade politician. What Barton does not know is that his car is booby trapped to explode as soon as he reaches fifty miles per hour.
Now read on.

Dick Barton had to slow the Riley Monaco as they came to a junction. Hetherington, the renegade ex-M.P. driving the Rolls Royce 20/25, had turned and was now speeding up again.

'Yes, I thought as much,' Dick Barton remarked. 'He's turning on to the Great North Road.'

From the back of the car, Jock Anderson was keeping an eye on the speedometer, it had risen to forty-three miles per hour, there was a worried look on his face.

'I don't like the sound of that engine, Mr Barton,' Jock said after a while.

The needle on the speedometer now read forty-five.

'Sounds all right to me,' Dick Barton replied. He kept watching Hetherington up ahead.

Forty-eight was now showing on the speedo.

'He'll show us a clean pair of heels unless we overtake him before the open road,' Barton stated. He was preparing to accelerate.

'Stop!' Jock Anderson's voice was filled with alarm.

'What the dickens are you talking about, Jock?' Though he questioned Jock's decision, Dick Barton had slowed down nevertheless.

Jock Anderson leant over the front seat. The urgency in his voice had increased. 'Will you stop the car, Mr Barton! Yon engine's been tampered with – I'd stake my life on it.'

'But we'll lose him,' Dick Barton protested.

'Never you mind that, sir,' Jock assured him. 'There's something going on under that bonnet I dinna like the sound of.'

Reluctantly, Dick Barton started to apply the brakes. 'Well, you're the boss in the engineering department,' he said.

The speedometer, which at its peak, had been touching forty-nine miles per hour, gradually dropped back.

The Riley stopped in the surburban street. Up ahead, the Rolls continued on its way. Barton, Jock and Snowey got out of the car. Immediately, Jock hurried round to the front of the car, and flung the bonnet open.

'There!'

Barton and Snowey followed the direction in which Jock Anderson was pointing. They could hardly miss what he was showing them. Strapped to the engine of the Riley were four sticks of dynamite.

'Well, well, well,' Dick Barton said grimly. 'Some sticks of rock. A present from Blackpool, no doubt.'

Snowey looked up at the special agent. 'More like a present from that Hetherington, if you ask me.'

'And with death printed all the way through,' Barton replied.

Jock looked up from where he was still examining the engine. 'It's wired up to the speedo, sir,' he told Dick Barton. 'As soon as you reached fifty . . .'

Dick Barton needed no help to reach the conclusion: 'Goodbye the old firm of Barton, White and Anderson.'

Jock had to admit that whoever had done the job had been of an ingenious turn of mind. 'It's neatly done,' he remarked to the other two.

'I'm glad to hear it,' Dick Barton said drily. Then he paused. 'Thank heavens for your Rolls Royce ear, Jock.' He became more serious. He couldn't fail to be aware of the fact that they had all missed death by just one mile per hour. 'Can you disconnect the thing?'

Jock bent over the engine once more. 'Och, yes!'

Snowey watched as Jock deftly began to feel his way amongst the maze of wires that connected the dynamite to the speedometer clock. Then, he turned to Dick Barton. 'Well, we've lost that Hetherington bloke, that's plain.'

Dick Barton looked up the long surburban street. Rows of neat houses stretched in a line to the horizon. There was no sign of the Rolls. 'Yes,' he agreed. 'It's back to Hampstead I think, Snowey. Miss Virginia's still in that cellar, remember?'

Already Jock Anderson was holding up a fistful of wires. It didn't look as if it would take him long to finish the job.

Back in the cellar of Hetherington's bijou Hampstead home, Curly Cohen, the bald headed thug, sometime chauffeur, and captor of Virginia and Rex Marley, was speaking into the radio receiver on the bare table in the smaller room.

'Stopped?' Curly was saying. 'What did he stop for, Guv?'

In the adjoining room, Virginia Marley was slowly working her way towards freedom. She was still gagged and bound, but as she leant against the brick wall of the cellar, she was slowly sawing at the ropes that held her against a staple that protruded from the wall.

As she worked, Virginia could hear the conversation that was going on over the radio receiver.

The sibilant tones of Melganik came over the receiver. 'Somehow he suspected our little device. Stand by the prisoner, Curly. In an hour we will move them up to GHQ.'

'In Wales, you mean?'

Melganik became angry. 'Quiet, you fool!'

'Sorry, Guv.'

But it was already too late for caution. Virginia had heard Curly give away the approximate location of the hideout. Her eyes narrowed as she thought what Dick Barton would give to hear the information. Then, from upstairs, she heard the doorbell ring.

When the French maid opened the front door of the house, she found herself looking once more at a working man in greasy overalls who was carrying a toolbag. But

70

this time there was a difference: there was someone else with him – the team was back in action.

'I got that spanner, Miss,' Barton said as he and Snowey stepped into the hall.

'Oh,' the maid replied in an irritated fashion. *'Sacre blue! Entrez.'*

'Brought my mate along in case I needed a hand,' Dick Barton explained.

'Comment?'

Barton pointed to Snowey. 'My mate. *Mon ami.'*

The maid seemed to have lost interest. 'Oh,' she replied. Then, she closed the door behind them, and after indicating the position of the ground floor bathroom, went off down the hall.

'Merci bien, mademoiselle,' Dick Barton said as she went away.

Then, Barton winked at Snowey, and together, they walked towards the bathroom. However, as soon as the maid was out of sight, they tiptoed hurriedly to the cellar door, and the special agent tried the handle.

Down in the cellar, Curly Cohen came back into the main room after speaking to Melganik. He looked suspiciously at Virginia, who in the meantime, had succeeded in freeing her hands, but still held them behind her back as if she was bound. Then, Curly glanced at Rex Marley. The crooner was still lying unconscious on the mattress in the corner of the room.

'Who was that at the door?' Curly Cohen wanted to know.

Virginia shrugged in ignorance. If she had been still tied, there would have been nothing else she could have done.

'I better check with the Guvnor,' Curly said to himself. He went back into the smaller room.

Virginia had watched as someone she knew came down the stairs. She was not, therefore, shocked when Dick Barton said: 'Hold it right there, Curly.'

But Curly Cohen's reaction was another matter altogether. He whirled around in surprise, and his hand immediately went into his bulging pocket. He produced a revolver, and was about to fire at Dick Barton when Virginia leapt at him, dragging his arm down so that Curly shot harmlessly into the cellar floor, and then dropped his gun.

'You she-cat,' Curly hissed.

But the thug was not yet outwitted. He turned and pulled the semi-conscious Rex Marley to his feet.

'The game's up, Curly,' Dick Barton stated flatly.

'So you think, Mr Clever Dick Barton,' Curly Cohen replied as he hoisted Rex Marley in front of him and began to back towards a heavy metal door set in the cellar wall.

Virginia Marley had discarded her gag, and now picked up Curly Cohen's gun. She pointed it at the thug, but dared not use it because she was afraid of hitting her brother.

Curly continued to back towards the wall. 'You're up against forces you couldn't even guess at,' he said to Dick Barton as he went. 'You're outclassed, Mr So-called Barton, and the sooner you realise it the better off you'll be.'

Curly Cohen disappeared through the opening dragging Rex Marley behind him. The heavy metal door shut with a clang. Dick Barton hurled himself against it, but his effort was futile.

'I wonder where in heaven's name that leads to?' the special agent muttered.

A buzz came from the next room as Snowey came down the steps. All three looked in the same general direction. The buzz came again.

'Seems impolite not to answer it,' Dick Barton said. He walked in and picked up the microphone, managing a passable imitation of Curly's voice.

'Curly here,' Barton said.

Meantime, Snowey White was helping Virginia to untie her ankles.

Melganik's voice came over the receiver. 'Curly – we've just learnt that Barton and his gang are on their way back to Mr Hetherington's house.'

'Don't you worry about that, Guv. I can deal with them,' Barton replied. He hoped his imitation was good enough.

'No!' Melganik's accent became more pronounced as

he got angry. 'You will take the prisoners and leave now for GHQ.'

'GHQ. Right you are, Guv. Where was that again?'

The voice at the other end of the receiver became furious. 'You dolt! At Llanech . . . ' There was a pause. Then Melganik seemed to recover his composure. 'That is not Curly,' he announced.

Dick Barton spoke in his own voice this time. 'No old chap,' he said. 'Barton's the name. Captain Richard Barton M.C., at your service.'

Melganik became furious once more. His accent was thick and foreign. 'Barton! Your impertinence and your irritating ubiquity is beginning to rile me!'

Dick Barton's reply was cool; 'I should learn English a bit better before you start on those long words, old son.'

There was an almost incomprehensible sound from the other end. It sounded like 'you'; Barton could not be sure. It was followed by a click as the receiver was switched off.

Barton grinned to himself. For a moment, he was one up. Though, naturally, there was still Rex to rescue. 'Excitable, these foreign chappies,' he said. Then, more directly to Virginia; 'You all right?'

'Just about,' Virginia replied. She was rubbing her wrists where the rope had chafed them. Snowey was standing by her side.

'Stout girl,' Dick Barton commented.

'Thanks,' Virginia said ruefully.

'I was referring to your spirit – certainly not your figure,' Barton said as he explained his compliment. 'Come on – let's get out of here.'

He led the way up the stairs. Snowey and Virginia followed.

Jock Anderson was sitting at the wheel of the Riley Monaco when he saw Dick Barton, Virginia and Snowey come out of Hetherington's house, and cross the road towards him. He got out of the car as they approached.

'No one tampered with the old flivver this time, I trust, Jock?' Dick Barton drew level with the car.

'They'd have had to cope with me if they'd tried, Mr Barton,' Jock answered.

Virginia and Snowey then approached. Barton made the introduction. 'Virginia – this is John Anderson, known to his friends as Jock for some unfathomable reason.'

Virginia smiled at the Scotsman. 'Hello, Jock – I hope I'm a friend.'

For the first time since Barton had known him, the mechanic seemed to be overcome with embarrassment. 'I'm sure I hope so too, Miss . . . '

'Marley – Miss Virginia Marley,' Barton said.

'Pleased to meet you, I'm sure.' Jock was now recovering. He grasped the handle of the back door of the car and held it open for Virginia. Then the others got in.

'You can drive if you like, Jock,' Barton said. 'We've got some hard thinking to do.'

The Riley Monaco pulled away from the Hampstead street.

As Jock concentrated on the driving, Dick Barton sat beside him in the passenger seat. Virginia and Snowey were in the back. The special agent's mind was on other things: 'Now we know that your brother's being taken to the headquarters of these crooks,' he said as he turned to face Virginia.

'In Wales.' Her reply was simple.

'In Wales?' Barton questioned.

'I overheard that Curly creature talking to Melganik about it,' Virginia explained.

'Melganik?' Barton wanted to know.

'That's the one who you were talking to on the radio,' Virginia shuddered involuntarily as she spoke. She hadn't liked the sound of the man's voice at all.

'Melganik's in on this, is he?' Barton commented.

'Yes. And a girl called Melissa Agranova.'

Barton spoke again: 'I don't know her.'

Snowey White didn't feel too comfortable. Even the mention of the woman's name reminded him of the bloomer he'd made.

'I think she's his fiancée,' Virginia took up her explanation again.

'I see.' A frown crossed Barton's face. When he spoke

74

it was with deliberation. 'If Dmitri Melganik is involved it's a dirtier game than even I imagined.'

Jock spoke directly to Barton. 'You know him do you, sir?'

'Indeed, I do, Jock.' Barton was looking out of the window as he spoke, but he was thinking about other, more foreign parts. Places where the streets of London seemed as remote as Timbuktu. 'I ran across him once in Istanbul. He was running a string of casinos but they were merely a front for some much nastier activities – white slavery – gun running – hired killings . . .'

'Sounds a bit of a bad boy to me, sir,' Snowey interrupted.

'Aptly put, Snowey,' came the reply. 'And not one to tangle with, I can assure you. Nonetheless we have no choice. So their headquarters is in Wales at Llanech . . . something.'

'Llanechbrantiog.' There was certainty in Jock's voice.

Dick Barton was very surprised. 'How on earth do you know that, Jock?' he asked.

Jock Anderson didn't take his eyes off the road. His attitude, like his skill at mechanics, was calm and precise. 'I been doing some thinking,' he said. 'I kenned as soon as I clapped eyes on it I'd seen that Hetherington's Rolls before. I mind I delivered it for somebody from Derby before the war – and that's where I took it to.'

Barton was pleased. He now had a definite lead on the unsavoury group of people connected with the master criminal. 'Then lead on, McDuff,' he answered.

Jock seemed unaware of the banter – at first. 'Anderson's the name sir,' he replied.

Barton spoke again: 'I was quoting the world's greatest poet, you ignoramus.'

'Never,' Jock said. There was a smile on his face. 'I know the works of Robbie Burns backwards.'

Barton smiled back. 'Drive,' he ordered. 'To Wales.'

Some hours later, Dick Barton and Jock were lying full length hidden in a clump of gorse amongst the wild, open moorland of North Wales. Barton was looking through his field glasses. A bleak range of hills stretched before him. The sky overhead was dark, and the hills were in shadow.

'That's Llanechbrantiog,' Jock said.

Through a rising mist, Dick Barton could just make out the posts of a tall barbed wire fence that ran across the side of the hill and disappeared into the distance.

'There was this great fence and a gate and I wasn't allowed to go through,' Jock continued. 'Some blokes met me. They didn't have proper uniforms or anything, but it was somehow like the army. That's why it stuck in my mind.'

Barton continued to scan right along the fence. It stretched for miles, following the dips of the hills as it went. 'There must be a way in somewhere,' he said. 'But I'm dashed if I can see it.'

Jock turned around to make sure that Snowey and Virginia were safe in the car, which was parked some distance behind them.

'There's the gate if you follow the road, of course,' Jock remarked.

Barton started to edge back through the gorse, towards the position of the parked car. 'Right. But that's guarded, you say. They're hardly likely to put the welcome mat out.'

Jock began to follow the special agent. 'No – I reckon not.'

'Mmm,' Barton murmured thoughtfully. 'This calls for a close reconnaisance.'

When Barton and Jock emerged from the gorse, they were beyond any point from which they could be viewed on the perimeter of the fence. They began to walk towards the Riley Monaco, it's black shape silhouetted against the surrounding hills.

'Any luck, sir?' Snowey asked when they were close enough.

' 'Fraid not, Snowey,' Dick Barton replied. 'We'll have to get in closer.' He looked at his watch. 'It's now . . . sixteen hundred hours.' He made a series of decisions: 'Snowey – you're coming with me. Jock – if we're not back by sunset – that's in about two hours – get to a telephone –

76

I noticed one in that village about five miles back. Call Detective Inspector Harrington at the Yard. Mention my name.'

'Right you are, Mr Barton,' Jock said promptly.

'Good lad. And keep a close eye on Miss Marley here.' As he spoke, Dick Barton turned towards Virginia.

Jock grinned in reply, and began to look embarrassed again. 'Och – that won't be too much hardship,' he said.

A more serious tone crept into Dick Barton's voice. 'We don't want her getting herself kidnapped again.'

'Over my dead body,' Jock declared.

Barton began to look over the hills. Dark, ominous clouds were forming on the horizon, seeming to signify that they were in for trouble. And not just with the weather. 'That's the ticket,' he said to Jock after a while. 'Now, frankly I don't know what the heck we're going to find behind that fence . . . '

'Nothing you and me can't handle, sir, I'll be bound,' Snowey interrupted from where he was standing.

A thoughtful expression crossed Dick Barton's face. 'Maybe. Maybe. But the first rule of war is – never underestimate your enemy.'

Snowey was feeling more sanguine about their chances than his former captain. But then he had yet to see the perimeter fence that stretched for miles across the otherwise bare moorland. 'Nor overestimate him, neither,' Snowey said. 'We learnt that outside Salerno, eh sir?'

'True,' Dick Barton agreed. 'Anyway – enough of the pep-talk. Let's go.' He turned to walk over the hills once more. 'Come on, Snowey.'

Virginia Marley watched her rescuer begin to stride into more possible danger. She was concerned about him. 'Good hunting, Dick,' she said as Barton and Snowey began to move.

Without looking round, Dick Barton waved cheerily in reply.

The special agent and Snowey White were hidden behind a boulder. All around them stretched undulating hills. In the valleys there were rough stretches of grass, and rushes marked out the boglands. But there, on the hilltops, it was barer. As far as they could see the sturdily built barbed wire fence stretched into the distance.

'It's a devil of a big area this fence encloses,' Dick Barton remarked.

'There's a break in the ground over there, sir,' Snowey pointed in the general direction.

'Where?' Dick Barton asked. He wanted a more specific location.

'See by that white rock-like triangle,' Snowey said.

'Got you.'

'Just about twenty yards beyond that.'

Dick Barton picked up his field glasses and trained them on the area that Snowey had mentioned. He could now see clearly that it was more than just a break in the ground. There were white scars on the hillside, evidence of other workings. There was a clear depression that had been man-made.

'Looks like the edge of a cliff or something, almost,' Snowey said as Barton looked through his glasses.

'Not exactly a cliff, Snowey,' Dick Barton said softly. 'A quarry.'

Dick Barton had seen enough. He put down his glasses, and looked closely at the barbed wire fence, thinking of a way that they could get through.

'If we only had some of them lovely wire cutters, sir,' Snowey remarked. 'Like what the Sergeant-Major used to cut his nails with.'

Dick Barton moved into a crouching position, and started to go cautiously forward. 'No good wishing for the moon, Snowey. Come on.'

So Dick Barton and Snowey left their cover, and darted over the open landscape. Remembering their commando training, they used whatever landscape features were available as a shield. Twice, they dropped down behind some bushes. And then they were on their way again, over the stony hilltop. They were now approaching the fence.

'Get down, quick!' Dick Barton whispered urgently.

They both dropped to the ground. A few moments passed. Then, Barton cautiously raised his head. His sixth sense had been right. When he looked up he saw a guard patrolling the fence. The man was Oriental. He was dressed in a quasi-military style uniform, and for company he had two large Alsatian dogs straining at their leashes. He was also wearing an armband that had an insignia Dick Barton recognised. It was the ideogram that had taken Mr Chen's breath away. The one, according to Snowey, that Melissa, Melganik's fiancée had been wearing on her brooch.

The Oriental guard, accompanied by his dogs, drew level with the spot where Snowey and Barton lay concealed. One of the dogs stopped and started to howl. The guard stopped and looked around suspiciously. When the dog howled again, the guard reached for his pistol.

Will Barton and Snowey be discovered before they penetrate the mysterious quarry? What lies behind the forbidding fence erected by Hetherington on these innocent Welsh hills?

Read the next chapter of: Dick Barton – Special Agent.

Chapter Seven

Dick, Jock and Snowey have succeeded in rescuing Virginia Marley from the cellar in Hampstead where Melganik and Hetherington were holding her captive. But they still hold her brother, crooner Rex Marley, and have taken him to a mysterious quarry in Wales. Barton and Snowey try to gain admittance to the quarry but find that it is heavily guarded.

Now read on.

The second Alsatian now joined the first, and they both began to whine in unison, and strain towards where Dick Barton and Snowey White lay concealed in the heather. All that separated the special agent and his friend from

79

discovery was a ten-foot high barbed wire fence.

'Sounds like Saturday night at the dog's home, don't it, sir?' Snowey said softly.

'As long as they don't imagine it's feeding time,' Dick Barton replied.

The tense moments ticked away slowly. Neither Barton nor Snowey dared to look up. Then they heard the guard say a few sharp words in a foreign tongue to the dogs. The whining subsided as the three formidable looking opponents moved away.

The ten-foot high barbed wire fence loomed up in front of them. At the top, it angled out slightly towards them. The guard was safely out of sight. Their problem was now more immediate.

'Climb it do you reckon, sir?'

Barton pointed to the angle at the top of the fence. 'Not with that overhang,' he said flatly.

And so, still at a crouch, they moved on. After, a while, it was Snowey's acute observation that provided them with a possible way in.

'Look,' he said.

Barton saw a slight depression in the ground, one which had possibly been caused by subsidence. There was a gap of approximately twelve inches between the lowest strand of wire and the earth.

'It's worth a try,' Dick Barton announced. 'Keep an eye open for the hounds of the Baskervilles.'

And with that, he began to wriggle under the gap in the fence while Snowey held the bottom up for him. As he gripped the barbed wire, ex-sergeant White looked keenly this way and that along the fence.

'How the humble grass snake gets around has always been a mystery to me,' Barton said, as lying on his belly, he worked his way through. Then he paused. 'Unhook the Harris tweed there, Snowey, will you?'

Carefully, Snowey did as he was asked. 'There you go, sir. All clear now.'

'Good man.' Dick Barton then continued to work his way along the ground, and, eventually, he cleared the fence.

'Now your turn, Snowey-me-lad,' he said when he was through.

Snowey was still on the other side of the barbed wire. 'I was afraid of that,' he commented as he looked down at the narrow gap. Then, with Dick Barton holding up the bottom strand for him, Snowey started his crawl.

'I think you've put on a bit of weight, Snowey, since your demob,' Barton said when Snowey appeared to be having some difficulty.

'You may have something there, sir,' came the reply. 'But it ain't from easy living.'

Soon, Snowey joined Barton on the inside of the fence. They crouched down together.

'Now the fun really starts. Come on, Snowey,' Barton said as he began to crawl forward towards the edge of the quarry. Snowey followed him.

'Cor lumme, guvnor.'

Dick Barton agreed with Snowey's expression of amazement, even if he would have put it with more aplomb. They were staring down into the quarry, after having made sure that they could not be seen. And what *they* could see was extremely sinister.

In the foreground stood another Oriental man. He was not the guard they had escaped from earlier, but was obviously of higher rank – possibly an officer. His uniform was covered with insignia, and his bearing indicated that he was used to authority. He was calling out an order in a foreign language. Dick Barton was too far away to catch the exact phraseology.

Behind the officer, a body of men were drawn up for inspection. Barton reckoned that there must be at least twenty of them. All were carrying arms and wore the same distinctive uniform, as if they had been stamped with approval by the renegade Hetherington and the arch criminal Melganik.

The officer walked up and down inspecting the men, making comments here and there. There was no lack of discipline, even if the intention behind their concealment in a disused quarry in North Wales was not exactly democratic.

6

In the background, behind the rows of armed Orientals, Dick Barton noticed several army lorries drawn up in a neat row. He turned to Snowey White and raised an eyebrow.

'Regular private army, if you ask me, sir,' Snowey commented.

'As well as being extremely sinister and strictly illegal under the Street Assemblies Act,' Dick Barton replied.

There was a pause before Snowey spoke again. 'You reckon this is where they brought that Mr Marley the crooner, sir?'

'That's exactly what we have to find out, Snowey,' Dick Barton said. 'First objective – get inside.'

Snowey glanced down at the activity taking place on the floor of the quarry. The formation of men lined up in front of the officer was beginning to break up. 'Easier said than done,' he remarked.

'I don't know about that,' Dick Barton answered. 'Look.' He pointed down to the quarry floor where Snowey had just been watching.

Some of the guards were taking up positions at the entrance to the quarry. But what was more interesting to Dick Barton was that another group of men were moving towards a vast iron door set in a fissure in the rock wall. It was on this door that he concentrated his attention.

'There's obviously something going on underground here, Snowey,' Barton said after a while. 'And that's the main entrance to wherever it takes place.'

Snowey was still dubious: 'No chance of getting in there, sir. Look at them blooming Chink guards.'

But Barton had already taken into account the armed Orientals on each side of the vast door. He was thinking of other possibilities. 'There must be another entrance, Snowey, however unorthodox.'

They both began to look around the immediate area. Snowey hoped that the governor was right. If he was, then it wouldn't be the first time.

Some distance back over the bleak hills, Jock Anderson sat at the wheel of the Riley Monaco, nervously drumming his fingers against the leather cover. Virginia Marley sat in the passenger seat beside him. There was a silence between them.

'What's the time, miss?' Jock asked after a while.

Virginia looked at her wrist watch. 'Five o'clock,' she replied.

Jock looked into the distance to see if there was any sign of Barton and Snowey. There was nothing, only a looming Welsh mist, and somewhere behind it, the sun was beginning to sink in the evening sky. 'They've been gone an hour now,' Jock muttered.

Virginia's anxiety showed more plainly: 'I do hope they're all right,' she said.

Jock turned in the driving seat so that he was facing Virginia. 'Mr Barton looks like a gentleman who can look after himself all right.'

'Oh yes!' Virginia agreed quickly. Then she paused before she spoke again. 'But it's got so much more complicated than it seemed at first. And dangerous.'

Once more, Jock Anderson peered out across the surrounding hills.

Dick Barton had found what he was looking for. His close scrutiny of the ground where he and Snowey were watching the activity in the quarry below had paid dividends.

'And this looks like it, Snowey my boy,' he announced.

Snowey didn't know what his ex-captain was talking about. 'What looks like which, sir?'

'Our unorthodox means of entry,' Dick Barton explained as he pointed to where, a few yards away, a concrete ring of about a foot high and a little wider in diameter was set into the ground. 'Man cannot live by bread alone,' the special agent continued. 'Not even Mr Charles Hetherington. He also needs oxygen.'

Snowey looked at the shaft. He reckoned it was about two feet wide. He wondered about it. Then, he looked up at Dick Barton. 'You think it's a ventilation-shaft like, sir?'

'Very like,' Barton replied. 'Come on.'

They began to approach the shaft. Leaning over the edge, Dick Barton peered down. He could hear a faint noise through the silence. 'Yes,' he said to Snowey. 'Listen.'

Then it was Snowey's turn to lean over the edge. Somewhere, very far away, there came the sound of something like machinery. 'Sort of humming noise,' he commented.

'Right,' Dick Barton agreed. 'An exterior fan unless I'm very much mistaken.' He pointed towards the shaft. 'How's your claustrophobia, Snowey?'

'Coming along nicely, thank you, sir.'

'Good,' came the reply. 'Come on then.' Dick Barton looked quickly around and began to lower himself into the shaft. It looked like being a tight fit.

Then, as Barton squeezed himself further into the shaft, he heard Snowey's voice from above: 'If you wouldn't mind just passing along the bus there, sir.'

'What's up?'

Snowey glanced once more over his shoulder, and he didn't like what he saw. The Oriental guard with the two Alsatians straining at the leash was about one hundred yards away. He didn't appear to have seen them – yet.

'Our chum with the dear little doggies is on his way round again,' Snowey answered.

Barton looked up quickly. 'I see what you mean, Snowey,' he said as his head disappeared. 'Come on in – the water's fine.'

Snowey misunderstood the quip. 'Water – too?' he began to complain. 'Oh well – nor more nor what I'd expect.'

Then, as the guard drew closer, Snowey also disappeared into the shaft.

Their progress was painful. Twice, Snowey barked his shins badly, and the rough concrete sides of the shaft weren't exactly easy on his hands, either. Still, Dick Barton was making his way ahead without complaining, as Snowey followed gamely on.

'We're in luck, Snowey,' Dick Barton announced from the darkness.

'You could have fooled me, sir.'

There was a pause. Then Barton's voice came again.

through the blackness; 'The shaft bends here and seems to go diagonally.'

Snowey wasn't beyond irony, even in the dark. 'Oh good,' he commented. 'Join the army and see the world; get demobbed and see the inside of a ventilation shaft under a ruddy quarry in the middle of nowhere.'

'Sshh!' Dick Barton's warning came through the darkness in the confined space.

Snowey glanced upward and saw the silhouette of the guard peering down the shaft. The Alsatian dogs were whining and growling somewhere up ahead.

Snowey squeezed himself around the bend and held his breath. After a while, he heard the sound of the dogs gradually fade into the distance. He let out a sigh of relief.

'I thought we were going to be a dog's breakfast for a minute,' he said to Dick Barton after the danger had passed.

'Not a pleasant thought, eh?' came the reply from up ahead. 'Let's get going.'

Once more, they resumed their painful progress along the shaft.

From the passenger seat of the Riley Monaco, Virginia Marley glanced out over the surrounding hills. There was no sign of Dick Barton or Snowey. The immediate landscape looked forbidding. There was no shelter or signs of civilisation anywhere on the hills. For a moment, she wished that she was back in the comfort of her father's London home.

She looked at her watch. 'They've been gone an hour and a half now Jock,' she said to the mechanic, who was still sitting by her side.

'Aye,' Jock replied thoughtfully. 'Will I go up yon rise and have a wee look?'

'No – don't leave me,' Virginia said. She was surprised by the intensity in her own voice. 'This place is beginning to give me the creeps.'

A glimmer of light attracted Dick Barton's attention. He stopped going forward along the shaft. He could hear Snowey still scraping his way along behind.

'Hold it, Snowey,' he said. 'We seem to have arrived somewhere.'

The noise of Snowey moving stopped. Dick Barton could feel his presence close behind. He now looked in the direction of the light. It came in squared patterns through the metal chequerboard of a ventilation grille set into the side of the shaft. He moved closer. The shaft itself continued on around a bend, but the grille looked out on to a corridor hewn from the living rock. The corridor itself curved sharply so that he could not see very far.

Even so, Dick Barton could make out a couple of metal doors set in the walls. For the moment, there was no one around. The corridor was deserted and silent except for the faint but pervasive hum of the ventilation system.

As he grasped the grille with both hands, Dick Barton said: 'If we can just shift this thing it may be our way in.'

From behind the ex-captain, Snowey could make out nothing at all. Dick Barton's shape blotted out the light. 'Pardon me for being so inquisitive, sir,' he said. 'But what thing?'

Barton shifted slightly to allow Snowey a glimpse of the object that he was talking about. 'Sorry, old son,' he replied. 'Forgot your view was somewhat restricted. There's a grille here leads into some sort of corridor.' A silence followed as he grabbed hold of the grille again. It began to shift slightly in its mounting. 'Ah . . . '

Dick Barton pulled at the grille once more. 'I think we're going to be in luck,' he told Snowey. Then the grille came away in his hands.

Darkness was beginning to come down over the Welsh mountains. Jock Anderson stood by the side of Dick Barton's car, looking anxiously in the direction of the Llanechbrantiog quarry, the hideout of master criminal Melganik, and the renegade Hetherington. There was no sign of Barton and Snowey.

Virginia Marley got out of the car and came over to stand beside Jock. Together, they walked over to the brow of a knoll from where they could get a better view of the quarry. No one came towards them. Virginia looked at her watch. She saw Jock look down towards her. They didn't speak.

The grey rock walls of the bare corridor stretched away on either side. There was a bare concrete floor, and nothing that indicated any activity – for the moment. Dick Barton watched alertly as Snowey White climbed down towards him. They took care to leave the metal grille in place. It was not their intention to inform anyone of their whereabouts.

'Well,' Dick Barton said as he glanced around the corridor. 'You pays your money and you takes your choice.'

'I'd say this way, sir,' Snowey replied as he pointed to the left. 'So far as I can get my bearings that seems to be the direction of those big doors in the quarry.'

'You may be right, Snowey,' Dick Barton said thoughtfully. Then, he held up a hand for silence.

Snowey listened carefully. From some distance away, he heard the sound of marching feet. The sound was coming towards them. He looked to where Dick Barton was standing.

'Our choices have become somewhat more limited than we'd imagined,' the special agent declared. He pointed towards one of the steel doors set in the wall. 'In here – quick!'

Dick Barton quickly grasped the handle of the metal door nearest to him. But it was of no use. The door was firmly locked. 'Try the other,' he said to Snowey.

Snowey did as Barton ordered. The door opened slowly. The room inside was dark, but there was no time to hesitate. They dived inside, and Dick Barton left the door open slightly so that he could see who was approaching.

The tramp of feet came nearer. And nearer. From his position, Barton could make out about a dozen Oriental soldiers in a double file. They passed so close that he could almost feel their breath. They were totally inscrutable, their faces expressionless. Each one wore the uniform with the ideogram on the armband. And each carried a sten gun.

With relief, Dick Barton watched the soldiers file slowly past. He turned to Snowey and spoke softly: 'Well, our oriental friends seem to have gone on their way.'

'Just as well, sir,' Snowey replied. 'Nasty blighters, if you ask me. Don't have the respect for human life like we do. Something to do with their religion, I daresay.'

Dick Barton agreed with the views expressed by his ex-sergeant. 'That and there being so many of them,' he said. Then, he paused and looked around in the dark. 'While we're here we may as well have a dekko. Seen anything of a light switch?'

Snowey's reply came out of the blackness. 'I ain't seen anything except the end of my nose for the last five minutes, sir. And even that's a bit dim.'

'Must be a switch somewhere,' Dick Barton declared. 'Feel around the door.'

And then, with startling suddenness, another voice cut through the darkness.

'Perhaps I can be of some assistance, Mr Barton?'

A blaze of light illuminated the room. For a moment, neither Barton or Snowey could make out anything at all. Gradually, they became accustomed to the new conditions. And found that they were formidable.

The room was a vast cavern hewn out of the rock. It would have been intimidating enough in its size alone. But, at the far end of the room were several occupants that made it even more so. The first of these was Hetherington, he was sitting on a chair on a raised dais. Behind him was a gigantic map of the British Isles that almost covered the wall. To his side were two guards with sten guns. The guns were pointed at Dick Barton and Snowey.

Glancing around the room, Dick Barton saw that there were other guards with guns. The direction in which they trained their stens was the same.

'Well, well, well,' Dick Barton said casually. 'We meet at last, Mr Hetherington.'

Hetherington rapped out an order to the guards in reply: 'Take them!'

Half a dozen guards began to advance on the special agent and his friend.

'Action stations, I think, Snowey, don't you?' Dick Barton said.

'Looks like it, sir,' came the reply. 'There's only half a dozen of them.'

The guards continued to advance.

Is this the end for Barton and Snowey? How can they escape from traitor Hetherington's underground lair?
   Read the next chapter of: Dick Barton – Special Agent.

Chapter Eight

Dick Barton and Snowey White, in their efforts to free Rex Marley, the drug-addict crooner, from the clutches of Dmitri Melganik, have penetrated the very heart of his sinister organisation – an underground complex in Wales at which the renegade M.P. Charles Hetherington trains his private army. Hetherington and his oriental guards are waiting for them . . .
   Now read on.

'Right!'
   Fists up in the classic Marquis of Queensberry manner, Dick Barton and Snowey stepped out to meet the first two of the advancing Oriental guards.
   Dick Barton delivered a straight right to the jaw to the guard nearest him. Snowey, who was proving to be slightly more adept in this combat, inflicted a right to an oriental solar plexus, and then floored his opponent with a left hook.
   Hetherington, who had been watching the struggle with a slightly amused expression on his face, now became more serious. He frowned as the other guards began to unsling their sten guns. 'No! I want them alive,' he ordered. Then, he turned to the two guards standing on either side of him. 'Heng, T'sien.'
   These two leapt down from the dais, discarding their guns as they did so. The other guards fell back, smiling smugly as they retreated.
   'Am I to take it that we're in for some sort of special

89

treat, Snowey?' Dick Barton said.

Snowey nodded towards the approaching combatants who came crouching forward in a martial arts style of fighting. 'Chop Suey maybe, sir,' he muttered. 'Looks like about all they're good for.'

The first guard had now reached Dick Barton and was attempting to grip him in a judo hold. The special agent feinted, then threw a straight left to the jaw. It connected. The Oriental called Heng grimaced with pain, then he backed away and prepared to come in again. Again, Dick Barton tried to throw a left. But this time he was not successful. Heng sidestepped the special agent, grasped his arm, and threw him to the ground.

From the floor, Dick Barton looked up speculatively at the looming figure of the guard. 'Ju-jitsu, eh?' the special agent muttered. 'Must have been taking a correspondence course, Snowey.'

'Still looks like a seven stone weakling to me, sir,' Snowey managed in reply, before T'sien was on him. Snowey grappled with the Oriental as best he could, but he was already too late. The other guards came from behind and pinned his arms to his sides. One glance told him that Dick Barton was in a similar position.

Overpowered, but still game, Dick Barton taunted the renegade M.P. 'Well – it took six of your yellow friends, Hetherington. Now what?'

Still sitting on his chair on the dais, Hetherington smiled slowly for a moment. Then he spoke: 'Don't be so impatient, Barton,' he said. 'Savour your last moments on earth – however unpleasant they might be.'

In the meantime, Virginia Marley and Jock Anderson had returned to the Riley Monaco. They now stood beside it. They both wore expressions of concern on their faces.

Not for the first time, Virginia looked anxiously at her watch. 'It's six o'clock,' she said to Jock.

'Right,' came the decisive reply.

Virginia, worried about Dick Barton and Snowey, was not keen to abandon her vigilance. She felt there was a chance they might still turn up. 'Do you think we ought to wait five more minutes?' she asked.

'No. No, Miss, I don't,' Jock Anderson said. 'If Mr Barton said six, he meant six. Can you drive a car?'

'Yes,' replied Virginia.

Plainly, Jock Anderson had not wasted his time while waiting for Dick Barton and Snowey to return. He now issued Virginia with crisp instructions. 'Right. You get down to the telephone in the village and call Detective Inspector Harrington at Whitehall 1212.'

Virginia opened the driver's door of the Riley, and began to get in. Then, turning to Jock, she said: 'What are you going to do?'

Already, Jock was beginning to walk in the direction of the quarry. Virginia noticed that he was carrying some tools with him. 'I'm going up to see if I can help,' Jock explained.

She watched as he moved further away from the car. 'Don't get into trouble, Jock.'

'Don't fash yourself about me, Miss,' the Scotsman said in return. 'Just get that call through.'

Virginia Marley settled herself into the driver's seat, turned on the ignition, and pressed the starter motor. The engine caught at once.

Dick Barton and Snowey, with their hands bound behind them, now stood against one of the walls of the cavernous underground room. The guards stood in front of them waving their sten guns menacingly.

Hetherington, who still sat on the dais, began to rant at them: 'Why do you try to stand against the march of history, Barton? Men like you – little men – with your pratings of "democracy" and "equality" – you think you can halt the advance of true progress?'

'No idea, old son,' Dick Barton's reply was deceptively casual. 'But if you're true progress I'll have a darn good try.'

Hetherington's face became red and angry. 'Quiet,' he ordered.

Once again, although his hands were bound behind him, and his back was literally to the wall, Dick Barton's coolness did not leave him. 'Sorry,' he said to Hetherington.

91

'I thought you were asking a question.'

The renegade M.P., the mind behind the vast complex in the Welsh mountains, and co-conspirator of the master criminal Melganik, leant forward in his chair. 'It is exactly your sort of little mind that tried to stop me before the war,' he declared to Dick Barton. 'I was willing to be reasonable; I was even willing to submit myself to the ludicrous procedure of putting myself up for the approval of the great unwashed. But the major political parties forced me to stand alone. Very well – stand alone I shall!'

'You and a few hundred chinks,' remarked Snowey White. He'd had enough of Hetherington. What with him going on all the time. Wouldn't even give a prisoner a chance to think of a way to escape.

Hetherington began to speak again. 'A few hundred? My dear Mr White, you sadly under-estimate me. What you have seen here is only a fraction of the power I have at my fingertips. I have bases the length and breadth of this island – each of them filled, as this one is, with men trained to take over the essential services of this country and run them as I command.'

Dick Barton was exasperated. 'Sieg-ruddy-heil,' he said to Hetherington. And he meant it.

Dusk was falling rapidly. The lonely country road across the North Wales moorland was not a very pleasant place to be. As she drove, Virginia Marley resisted the temptation to shiver. She had a job to carry out. She kept her eyes on the road.

It was lucky that she did, she thought, for the Riley's headlamps suddenly picked up a large American car that was parked right across the middle of the narrow road. She pushed her foot down hard on the brakes, and managed to stop only inches from the other vehicle.

She opened the door and got out. She was furious. 'What on earth do you think you're . . . '

And there Virginia Marley trailed off in mid-sentence, for, as the driver's door of the large American car opened, she found herself staring into the barrel of a revolver. The gun was held by someone she recognised – Curly Cohen.

'You,' Virginia said.

'Me. That's right,' Curly replied. His voice was quiet.

Then Virginia saw that the rear window of the car was being wound down. She also knew the figure who leaned out. He had a sinister scar and a sibilant voice. It was no one else but Melganik, the master criminal.

'We meet again, Miss Marley,' Melganik said. 'What a very great pleasure.'

'The pleasure is entirely yours, I can assure you,' Virginia retorted hotly.

Melganik's reply was almost a soft purr – except for the tinge of menace. 'I am so desolate to hear that,' he said. 'But perhaps you would care to join your brother in the car with me?'

'Rex?' Virginia took an involuntary step forward, and then, remembering what had happened last time, she stopped. 'No!' Her declaration was firm. 'I'm not being caught like that again, Mr Melganik!'

The master criminal shrugged as if it was a matter of no great importance to him. 'Trapped or not, my dear,' he remarked. 'You are coming with me.' He turned towards the thug in his employment. 'Get her, Curly!'

'Right!'

Curly Cohen took one quick pace forward and grabbed Virginia's arm. As he twisted it behind her back, the girl cried out in pain. 'Just don't make any trouble, miss, that's all,' the thug advised. 'Then nobody won't get hurt.'

Virginia tried to wriggle free but the pain was too great. She gave up her attempt at resistance as Curly Cohen pushed her towards the car. Melganik opened the rear door. He had a smile on his hideous face.

Virginia Marley was bundled inside.

Meanwhile, back in the cavernous underground room, the nerve-centre of Hetherington's operations in the remote mountains of North Wales, the renegade was still ranting at Dick Barton and Snowey White who were still pinioned against the wall.

'The decadence that has infected every aspect of life in this country must be removed – with the surgeon's knife if necessary. The culture that produced the nigger music performed by such pitiable objects as your friend Rex Marley must be restyled.'

Snowey White shrugged, then turned to Dick Barton who was standing by his side. 'He does go on, sir, don't he?'

The remark did not go unnoticed by Hetherington. His eyes were now glaring, and his face was flushed with anger. 'And you – you Barton, and you White. You who seek to uphold and defend the corruption in which we are forced to live – you must be among the first to go!' Hetherington paused for his words to take effect. 'I am not by nature a merciful man,' he resumed. 'Your demise will be slow – slow and hideously painful.'

Dick Barton timed his retort impeccably; 'You're going to bore us to death?' he suggested.

The ex-M.P. who did not regard democracy as the true condition of England, laughed in reply. 'Ah – you think you can joke, Mr Barton. But I think the smile will be on the other side of your face when you see what I have in store for you.'

As Hetherington stopped speaking, a deathly hush filled the underground room. Snowey White glanced towards Dick Barton, but the special agent's expression gave away nothing at all. Snowey began to wonder how – and if – the governor was going to be able to get them out of this one. All things considered, it was beginning to look very nasty.

Night had fallen on the mountains. As Jock Anderson crawled towards the perimeter fence that surrounded the quarry at Llanechbrantiog, he could hear the occasional owl in the distance. It was becoming cold, and with the blanket of darkness had come an enveloping dampness. But Jock had no time to think of his own predicament, it was very likely that Dick Barton and Snowey White were in trouble, and if he could, he meant to get them out of it.

Jock ducked as a searchlight beam swung over his head. He could make out a wooden guard tower of the kind used in concentration camps, it was quite near. Further away, but not so far that he couldn't see what was going on, was the main gate where he had left the Rolls-Royce 20/25 when he had delivered it from Derby before the war.

The searchlight swept over him again. Jock continued to lie low for what seemed a frighteningly long time. Then, it moved on.

He crawled on towards the fence, and, when he had reached it, extracted a pair of wire cutters from his pocket. He then began to snip at the first strands of barbed wire.

The sound of a car horn drew his attention. He stopped work for a moment, and watched the activity at the gate. An American car drew up, it was too dark for him to be sure of the model. Two guards standing near swung the gates open, and the car glided through. Then, the guards resumed their alert posture, and Jock went on with his work at the fence. It was lucky that he had a good pair of cutters.

One of the doors to the underground room crashed open, an Oriental guard entered, and then stood aside as two more important figures came in. They were none other than Dmitri Melganik and his fiancée Melissa.

'Ah, Dmitri,' Hetherington greeted the master criminal. 'I don't think you've met Mr Barton?'

Melganik directed his attention towards where Barton and Snowey were standing against the wall. He smiled, when he spoke it was with slow and sinister tones. 'We've spoken on the telephone.'

Hetherington continued his charade of courtesy. He indicated Snowey: 'And Mr White?'

'A lump.'

'Indeed,' Hetherington replied.

Snowey was indignant. He didn't like to be reminded of his mistake. 'Ruddy nerve,' he said. Then, he pointed to Melissa, he had recognised her the moment she had come through the door. 'She's the one, sir,' he said to Dick Barton. 'She's the one who pretended to be Mr Marley's fiancée and then got me clouted on the head.'

Melissa was not unaware of Snowey's identity. 'Ah,' she replied. 'It's poor Mr White of the delicate cranium.'

A more serious expression came over Melganik's face. 'Enough of this banter,' he declared. 'Bring in the other two.'

In obedience to Melganik's order, two more guards came

95

into the room. Virginia Marley was struggling valiantly with the first of them, but he was much too strong for her. Her brother Rex was still in no condition to resist. He was barely conscious. His face still had the deathly pallor that had marked him when Dick Barton had first seen the crooner at the *Blue Parrot*. And that seemed a long time ago.

Virginia and Rex were forced to join Barton and Snowey against the wall.

'Ah – we now have the complete set,' Hetherington remarked. He turned towards Melganik. 'Well done, Dmitri.' The master criminal smiled back at him.

Dick Barton spoke very quietly to Snowey: 'They seem to have overlooked Jock.'

But Snowey was dubious of the mechanic's chances. 'I don't know what he's going to do against this lot,' he said. He looked around the room. They were vastly outnumbered. The odds were stacked against them.

Jock Anderson had reached the edge of the quarry. Carefully, in case he should disturb any loose stones, and so give warning of his presence, the mechanic looked over the edge. And what he saw took his breath away. He had not expected anything like this.

There were several rows of troop lorries parked in well-ordered lines. Guards in Oriental uniform moved about in a seemingly efficient manner. The whole place gave the impression of a well ordered military operation. He was obviously going to have his work cut out. He let out a long, low whistle.

Dick Barton, Snowey White, Virginia Marley and her brother Rex, stared at the sten guns of the Oriental guards in the control of Hetherington and Melganik. For the moment, even Barton felt sure, there was nothing they could do – except play for time.

Hetherington, now obviously more relaxed, and with apparent contempt for his prisoners, was talking to his co-conspirator as he stood in front of them.

'Mr Barton here doubts the feasibility of our aims, Dmitri,' Hetherington said.

The master criminal smiled to himself. 'Of course he does,' he remarked. 'But then he doesn't yet know my half of the plan, I imagine?'

A self-satisfied smirk crossed Hetherington's face. 'I was about to move on to that.' He looked across to where Dick Barton was standing.

The special agent could stand no more. It was time for him to declare himself. He addressed himself to the master criminal. 'Anything you dream up, Melganik,' he declared, 'is bound to be dirty, but scarcely guaranteed to be successful.'

The equilibrium of the mid-European with the sibilant voice was not disturbed. 'Oh, I don't think that even the brilliant Mr Barton will be able to find a weakness in my scheme.'

Shrewdly, Dick Barton asked a key question: 'And what's that when it's at home?'

Melganik paused before he spoke again. 'It is quite simple really.' He seemed to hold the special agent's intelligence in contempt. 'I daresay our little raid on the tobacco warehouse from which nothing appeared to have been stolen had you bemused, huh?'

But there was a limit to the amount of inferiority that Dick Barton could pretend to. Even when his life was at stake. 'Not at all,' he replied. 'A child could see through it.'

'Indeed.'

'Indeed,' Dick Barton repeated. 'The bales of tobacco *were* stolen.'

'But they were checked and double checked by the great Detective Inspector Harrington of Scotland Yard, Mr Barton,' came the reply.

The special agent felt that there was now no point in concealing what he had worked out long ago. When his back was to the wall, the only thing to do was speak out. 'Yes,' Dick Barton said. 'What he didn't realise was that the dozen bales that you stole were replaced by a dozen seemingly identical bales.' He paused for a moment. 'Only they contained not innocent tobacco but marijuana.'

Melganik seemed unperturbed. He nodded his head as he spoke. 'Very good. Very good. And then?'

Dick Barton looked around at the group with him. Snowey had a determined expression on his face. Virginia was looking after Rex, whose condition had not improved since he had been brought into the room. They might all be at the master criminal's mercy, but he had no intention of showing fear. 'You tell me,' he said after a while.

'Ah – not so clever, after all.' Melganik now seemed to think that his scheme had gone far beyond the comprehension of the special agent and his friends. 'You have failed to think it through. I am a businessman, Mr Barton. What do I gain by substituting a very expensive drug for a few comparatively cheap dried leaves of the tobacco plant, Nicotiana Tobacum?'

'That's rather obvious, I'm afraid,' Dick Barton replied.

Virginia Marley looking up from her brother's slumped body, cried out indignantly; 'He wants to turn the whole population into drug addicts!'

Melganik nodded sagely. 'The young lady has brains as well as beauty,' he said. 'What a tragedy that the world will have the benefit of them for so short a time.' Even though he was uttering the most terrible threats, his voice carried the same silken tones as before. 'You see . . . ' he resumed.

From the dais, Hetherington interrupted. 'That's enough Dmitri,' he warned.

But the master criminal was far too egotistical to be prevented from telling the whole dastardly scheme. 'No, no,' he protested to Hetherington. 'Why should they not hear the whole thing? The grand design? It would be wanton cruelty to send them to their deaths not knowing for what they die. The look of puzzlement on their little faces would melt the stoniest heart.'

It was time to speak up again, Dick Barton decided. 'No puzzlement here, I assure you,' he stated.

'Oh indeed?'

There was no menace in Dick Barton's reply. When he spoke it was with a matter-of-fact certainty. 'I know all I need to know, Melganik,' he said. 'Enough to get you put away from the company of decent folk for the rest of your life.'

Snowey White watched Melganik's reaction. The governor had hit home all right. The mid-European was trying hard to keep up the pretence that he was still as cool as a cucumber in an iceberg. But Snowey noticed that Melganik's scar was beginning to become red with anger.

'Possibly,' Melganik said as he replied to Dick Barton's last remark. 'If you were in a position to make what you know public, which is hardly the case. But I digress.' He paused before he launched into a further speech, relishing the prospect of performing before a captive audience. 'Yes, of course the prospect of a population of hashish smokers is one to gladden the heart of he who controls the supply of that substance. But my colleague Mr Hetherington goes further. Once we have the wits of the populace suitably dulled, he will be in an ideal position to make his move to seize all means of communication within the capital and bend the country to his will.'

Even Dick Barton was stunned for a moment. The immensity and sheer coldbloodedness behind the evil scheme took his breath away. When he spoke it was with a softness that was full of hate: 'You unspeakable swine,' he said.

Melganik shrugged. 'Sticks and stones, Mr Barton – mere sticks and stones.'

Then the master criminal turned towards the guards. His tone became officious and cruel. 'Take them to the room,' he said simply.

The guards gathered around Dick Barton, Snowey White, Virginia Marley, and her still unconscious, drug addicted brother. Prodding them with their sten guns, they roughly bundled them through one of the steel doors, and into the corridor.

The rough treatment continued until the group reached another door set into the solid rock. The guards opened it, forced their prisoners inside, and then slammed the door behind them.

It was a small room, completely devoid of furniture. The walls were made of metal, and the place was illuminated by a single bare electric light bulb hanging from the ceiling. As the door slammed behind them, Dick Barton, who was supporting Rex Marley, propped him gently against one of the walls.

Outside, the tramp of feet receded. They were now alone, and left to whatever horrible death Melganik and Hetherington had devised.

Snowey turned towards Dick Barton. 'What now sir, do you reckon?'

There was a grim expression on the special agent's face. 'Something hellish, I have no doubt,' he muttered. Then, he looked to where Virginia was standing. 'Did you get through to Inspector Harrington?' he asked.

Virginia shook her head. 'I was on my way to telephone when they caught me.'

'So we can expect no help from that quarter,' Dick Barton commented. He looked around the room. The prospect was forbidding.

'I'm sorry, Dick,' Virginia said. She was upset.

Gallant as ever, Dick Barton did his best to keep morale high. 'Not your fault old girl. Keep your pecker up.'

'Jock's still free,' Virginia said hopefully.

At that moment, the single electric lightbulb flickered. Then, mysteriously, it brightened again.

'Hello – what's that?' There was alarm in Snowey's voice.

Then, from somewhere beyond the walls, there was the hum of an electric generator.

Virginia cried out suddenly: 'Something's happening – look!' She pointed towards the steel walls.

Dick Barton and Snowey looked at the wall. What they could see was unmistakeable. A regular pattern appeared. There were spots set six inches apart. The spots began to move towards them.

'What the . . . ?' Dick Barton's surprise showed in his voice. But he was still thinking quickly. 'Snowey,' he said, 'Get Mr Marley away from that wall – quick!'

Immediately, Snowey White obeyed instructions and hoisted the crooner to his feet. Then, he brought him towards the centre of the room.

'Well,' Dick Barton said. 'Friend Hetherington promised us something nasty and for once he's as good as his word.'

'What do you mean?' Virginia said in alarm. 'What is it?'

Dick Barton took a short step across the room towards

100

the nearest walls. He reached up to examine the 'spots'. It was apparent that they were far more dangerous than even he had first thought. They were now protruding into the room and advancing slowly towards the occupants.

'Solid stainless steel, my dear,' the special agent said. 'And each one with a tip like a razor.'

Virginia Marley gasped with fear.

But, even as Dick Barton spoke, the stainless steel rods with their tips of death were advancing further. They were now sticking out six inches and still moving.

Dick Barton glanced up at the ceiling. It was the same story from that direction. And the ending spelt out 'doom' quite clearly.

'Leaves nothing to chance, our Mr Hetherington,' he commented.

Time turned into inches of death for the group of four in the small steel room as the rods continued their advance. Twelve inches passed . . . eighteen inches . . .

They huddled in the centre of the available space.

'Dick – what can we do?' Virginia Marley was on the point of breaking down.

The special agent's voice was cool, but his heart and mind were racing. 'I don't know Virginia, I tell you – I just don't know.'

The pointed rods continued their inexorable advance.

How can Barton and Snowey protect Virginia and her brother from the deadly steel trap that is advancing on them?

Can Jock help?

Or has he, too, been captured?

Read the next chapter of: Dick Barton – Special Agent.

Chapter Nine

Dick Barton and Snowey, trapped with crooner Rex Marley and his sister Virginia in an underground cell, wait helplessly as a deadly network of stainless steel spikes advances inexorably upon them ...
Now read on ...

The whirring of the generator continued, and with each turn of the pistons, death was brought closer for Dick Barton, Snowey White, Virginia Marley, and her brother Rex. They were now huddled in the centre of the room as the stainless steel points came ominously closer.

'Well,' Dick Barton remarked grimly, 'Saving a miracle, this looks like it, chaps.'

Virginia Marley's face was once again strained with fear. 'Oh, Dick,' she said. 'Isn't there anything we can do?'

Dick Barton looked frankly at Virginia. 'Not a blessed thing, old girl.' He turned to his loyal ex-sergeant. 'Any ideas, Snowey?'

Snowey looked up and across at the network of steel that threatened to engulf them all. 'Not one that'll get us out of this little lot, sir, and that's a fact.'

The whir of the generator continued.

Outside the underground complex, braving the chill night air, and the greater danger of an almost certain fall to his death, Jock Anderson, former Rolls Royce mechanic, and currently the only member of the Dick Barton team who held a chance of saving his comrades, was climbing down the sheer rock face of the Llanchbrantiog quarry.

And inside the cavernous underground room, nerve-centre of an operation designed to take over the whole of the country, and in front of a giant map, the renegade M.P.

Hetherington was poring over charts with the master criminal Melganik, and his attractive but deadly fiancée Melissa.

'My information is that our drugged cigarettes will leave the factory, here,' Melganik said as he pointed out the location on the chart, 'and will be on sale in tobacconists all over the metropolis by the morning.'

Hetherington looked across the table to where his co-conspirator was standing next to Melissa. 'Well done, Dmitri.'

Melganik smiled. 'Planning and foresight, my friend,' he remarked. 'With these qualities anything can be achieved – anything! As you yourself well know.'

Hetherington reached up and patted down a stray hair that had come out of place. 'Yes – I think it would not be immodest to say that it is partly the attributes you have named that have achieved for me the position I hold today.'

Melissa smiled graciously at the ex-M.P. 'You are un-usual for an Englishman,' she said flatteringly. 'The English love the amateur – the good loser.'

A look of scorn crossed the once-elegant features of the Englishman who faced her across the table. 'Losers! I have nothing but contempt for losers – good or bad or indifferent. Mr Dick Barton is the supreme example of the blundering, misguided, stupid Englishman.'

Melissa's reply was quiet and final: 'We have no need to concern ourselves with him any more.'

'No indeed,' Melganik agreed.

Back in the room of death, Dick Barton and his accomplices were preparing to share their last minutes with each other. It seemed as if their time had finally come.

'I don't like the look of this, Mr Barton,' said Snowey White.

Dick Barton reached out and touched one of the spikes with the forefinger of his right hand. 'Nor me, Snowey,' he said. 'But at least friend Hetherington can't say he didn't see the point.'

Virginia Marley was amazed. 'How can you make jokes at a time like this?'

The Special Agent glanced at the approaching death

that advanced on them. There's very little else we can do I'm afraid, Ginny!'

'And don't call me Ginny.'

It was now Barton's turn to be surprised. 'Why not?' he asked. 'It's what I used to call you when you were a kid.'

Virginia looked closely at Barton. Really she thought, he showed no sign of fear at all. 'You may not have noticed it,' she said defiantly, 'But I'm not exactly a kid anymore.'

'I'd noticed it,' Snowey White chipped in. He was only telling the truth, after all.

Virginia smiled charmingly at him. 'Thank you, Snowey,'

Jock Anderson reached the quarry floor safely. No guards were near. Finding himself in the shadow of a long, sleek shape that he recognised, the mechanic advanced towards Hetherington's Rolls Royce 20/25.

In the operations room, Melganik straightened up from the chart table. 'So,' he said to Hetherington. 'Your forces can start their move on London now.'

The renegade M.P. with a disliking for democracy picked up a telephone receiver that was lying on the table. When he spoke, it was in the same Oriental language that the guard had used earlier. He barked a series of commands.

Melganik nodded with satisfaction as he watched Hetherington go through his paces. Then he glanced at his watch. 'By mid-day tomorrow they will have taken control of Broadcasting House, Northolt Aerodrome, and the main line stations. Also Scotland Yard.'

'And by midnight, the country will be ours!' The comment came from a very excited Melissa.

'Ours indeed, my little one,' Melganik chuckled.

Hetherington was disturbed by their exchange. 'Yours, Melganik?' he said.

To cover his slip, Melganik smiled broadly at the M.P. 'All three of us, of course Charles. The three of us, huh?'

Hetherington assumed what was intended to be a firm posture. There was authority in his voice; 'Only one man can control the destiny of a nation,' he remarked.

'Of course, of course, the master criminal assured him. 'But even you will need advisers – associates,' he corrected himself in time.

'Advisers, possibly,' Hetherington conceded.

Jock Anderson closed the bonnet of the Rolls Royce, and moved further into the shadow provided by the quarry wall. He stopped for a moment as he heard the crunch of approaching feet, and, flattening himself into a fissure in the rock, kept hidden until a guard walked past.

Then, when he was sure that it was safe, the mechanic began to work his way towards the vast steel doors that led into the underground complex. He paused thought-fully as he noticed the guards on either side of the en-trance.

But, nearer, there was something that looked more promising. There was a much smaller door, also made of steel, that bore the inscription – 'KEEP OUT! DANGER! ELECTRIC GENERATOR!'

For a moment, Jock listened outside the door. Sure enough, a steady hum came from within. Then he tried the door handle. It was not locked. Allowing himself a faint smile, he opened the door, went in, and closed it behind him.

The stainless steel spikes were now almost upon them. There was no room to turn around. It seemed as if Dick Barton, Snowey White, Virginia Marley and her brother would be locked in their present positions for eternity.

'Well, Snowey-me-lad,' Dick Barton said, 'we've been through a lot together . . . '

'Now it looks as if a lot's going to go through us,' Snowey quipped in reply.

Dick Barton looked closely at his ex-sergeant. 'Well said, Snowey, that's the spirit.'

Suddenly, the bare electric light bulb that illuminated the room flickered and then went out.

Snowey's voice echoed in the darkness; 'Now what?'

Virginia Marley finally broke down. 'It's that awful

Hetherington man,' she screamed. 'He's going to make us die in the dark!'

A quiet voice tried to calm her. Thoughtfully, Dick Barton said: 'No – I don't think so. Listen.'

For a moment, there was no sound at all in the small steel room. Not even the hum of the generator.

'I can't hear anything,' Virginia said after a while.

'Precisely,' Dick Barton answered. His deduction had proved correct. 'Remember we could hear the hum of a motor before? There's been an electrical failure – and this charming little death-trap was worked electrically.'

Snowey breathed an audible sigh of relief into the darkness. 'I think you're right, guv,' he said.

By Snowey's side, Virginia Marley made a little nervous movement. 'But we still can't get out,' she complained.

In the moments of respite from a horrible lingering death, Dick Barton's brain had been working furiously. And, as usual, he had come up with a possible solution. 'Or can we?' he asked. Snowey was still standing in the dark beside him. 'Snowey, old son,' Barton suggested, 'I know you've gained a pound or two since the military lost your services . . . '

It was a sore point with ex-sergeant White. 'No need to go on about it sir,' he said.

Dick Barton continued with his suggestion: 'Do you think you could wriggle under the bottom spikes and get to the door?'

Snowey considered the suggestion for a moment. It was going to be difficult. He couldn't even see his hand in front of him. Still, he didn't really have much option. 'I can have a go, sir,' he replied.

Barton's crisp tones came through the darkness: 'Then do that small thing.'

There was darkness all around him. The moon was low, and covered by cloud shadow. When Jock Anderson stepped out of the generator room he could hear confused shouting in the distance. The floodlighting in the quarry had gone out when he had tampered with the generator. The shouting continued, and then, he heard the sound of a single pair of footsteps running towards him.

Jock waited in the darkness until the footsteps were level with him, then, he extended a foot and the guard went flying. The Oriental was quick to recover, he leapt up and unslung his sten gun. But the mechanic downed him again with an uppercut to the jaw. Then he bent down and picked up the gun.

Feeling his way slowly through the darkness, and taking care in case he should impale himself on the stainless steel spikes, Snowey White felt his way towards the door that would lead out of the room of death.

'Well, here I am, sir,' he said to Dick Barton when he had reached the end of the room. 'Now what?'

'Can you reach the lock?' Dick Barton wanted to know.

In the blackness that surrounded him, Snowey felt for distinguishing features on the door. He found the handle, and then, just below it, made out the shape of the lock. 'Just about ,' he muttered in reply.

'Can you pick it?'

'Cor stone my grannie's hat,' Snowey exclaimed. He'd been asked to do some strange things in his time, but this one was really the limit. Even so, he groped once more into the darkness, trying to discover what kind of a lock it was.'

Tensely, Dick Barton waited as he heard scrabbling in the blackness.

'It don't feel too bad, sir,' Snowey said after a while.

'Have a shot at it,' Barton suggested.

Snowey thought for a while. Then, he said to Virginia: 'You wouldn't have a hairgrip, Miss, would you?'

Surprised, Virginia Marley took her time in answering. 'Why – yes,' she replied.

Snowey's cockney accent came through the darkness once more:

'Do you think I could have a lend of it?'

The cavernous underground room, operations centre of a dastardly plan, was now lit only by flickering candlelight. Hetherington stood by the table. He was speaking into the telephone. He was extremely agitated.

'Then mend the generator,' he shouted. 'What? Where? Deal with it.'

He slammed the phone back down on to the receiver and then turned to Melganik and Melissa who were standing nearby. 'The generator has been sabotaged,' he announced.

'Sabotaged?' There was puzzlement in Melissa's soft, purring voice.

'And one of the guards knocked unconscious and tied up,' Hetherington finished. He was angry.

A frown crossed the features of the master criminal Melganik.

'Who could do this thing?' he wanted to know. 'The only outsiders who know of our plans are safely ensconced in our room of death.'

A tense pause followed as Hetherington considered the situation. He glanced warily at Melganik and the attractive but deadly woman by his side. 'Unless . . . ' he began.

Melganik's reply was swift. 'Unless what?'

Hetherington's urbanity returned. He was now in complete control of himself once more. 'Unless, my dear Dmitri, this is not the work of an outsider – but sabotage from the inside.' He paused to let the implications behind his words sink in. 'What General Emilio Mola first called a fifth column.'

'Preposterous.' Melganik's accent showed thickly.

'Is it, though?' Hetherington continued in totally relaxed fashion. 'The plan is made, the troops trained, the orders given. Nothing can stop it now.' He paused again. So perhaps someone thinks he can take advantage of the work I have done and take over – quietly disposing of me in the process.'

'I don't know what you're implying . . . ' Melganik began.

Hetherington reached in the jacket pocket of his well-cut suit, produced an automatic pistol and stepped back. 'I think you do, Dmitri,' he said quietly.

'You fool!' Melganik shouted back at him.

'Not such a fool as you take me for,' Hetherington said coldly. 'You and your mistress.'

'How dare you!' Melissa stepped forward in outrage.

Hetherington waved the automatic in her direction 'Oh – I dare, my dear – I dare. You think I haven't watched you plotting together, whispering in corners, exchanging glances, giving orders to my men that you have no right to give?'

'This is sheer madness,' Melganik protested.

The renegade M.P. covered them both with the gun. 'Madness, is it? When you and this Agranova woman talk about being my "associates." '

For once, it was the master criminal's turn to taste fear. He saw the cold glint of determination in Hetherington's eyes. He did his best to mollify him: 'Advisers, my dear Charles, is what we said.'

Hetherington's voice rose in anger. 'You think I need advice from you? You think that I,' he puffed out his chest, 'a man trained in the whole spectrum of political skills – a leader born of a line of leaders stretching back to the Conqueror – need advice from a man conceived in the stews of Trieste and raised in the gutters of Alexandria?'

Melganik could no longer contain himself. His intelligence and capability had been questioned. His giant ego had been bruised. 'Why you . . . ' he began, as he advanced towards his former partner.

But the master criminal got no further than his first step. Totally in control of himself, Hetherington pressed the trigger of the automatic. With the first shot, Melganik staggered backwards, his hands to his chest.

'You... fool...' he gasped.

But, with the second shot, Melganik collapsed on his knees, and then fell sideways to the ground. His body contorted, and then went rigid. His eyes open, staring.

Melissa rushed to the aid of her accomplice, and crouched down beside him. She paused a moment, then she looked up at Hetherington. 'He's dead,' she said quietly. 'You've killed him.'

Dick Barton's cigarette lighter flickered in front of him as he held it out to provide light for Snowey to work by. The cockney ex-sergeant was working on the door lock with a hair grip that he had borrowed from Virginia Marley.

'How goes it, Snowey?' Barton was careful to keep the

lighter held as high as he could. Snowey would want as much light as possible.

Snowey thrust the hairpin into the tumbler mechanism once more. 'Bit dodgey, sir,' he said quietly.

Virginia spoke from her position close to the two friends. 'Supposing they start the electricity again.'

'We'll cross that bridge when we come to it,' Dick Barton said. He wondered how much fuel he had left in his lighter.

Progress was not as fast as Jock Anderson had hoped. Twice, he had to flatten himself against the quarry wall as guards ran past towards the generator room. This time, after eluding them yet again, he went quietly in the direction of the main doors that led underground. He was in luck; a group of four guards stood in front of the open doors, jabbering excitedly in Chinese, and pointing up towards the non-functioning searchlight set above the door.

Making as little noise as he could, Jock sidled past them. He was not noticed. He had gained entry to the underground complex.

The moments ticked by slowly as Snowey repeatedly inserted the hairgrip into the lock's mechanism. There was absolute quiet as he listened for the tumblers to fall into place. Then, there was a quiet 'click'.

'Got it!' came the triumphant shout.

'Good man, Snowey,' said Dick Barton.

The petrol lighter still flickered. Snowey gently began to open the door.

'Now comes the difficult part,' Dick Barton announced.

Virginia kept her position in the dark, cold room. Something else was on her mind. 'How are we going to get Rex under the spikes?' she asked.

'Exactly,' the special agent replied. 'If we could just get to the other side we could drag him, I suppose.' He glanced at the network of steel that separated him from Snowey White. 'You get out into the corridor anyway, Snowey, and keep your eyes peeled.'

110

'Right, sir,' Snowey answered. He began to squeeze his way through the spikes that still blocked his escape.

But, little known to Jock Anderson, the group of Orientals that had rushed into the generator room had already finished their repair work. From inside the room, came a series of comments in Chinese. Then, the generator started up again.

And, as the motor hummed, in the small steel room, the single electric light bulb came on again, and the deadly spikes began their advance once more.

'Snowey!' There was urgency in Dick Barton's voice.

Snowey White stopped dead in his tracks and peered around the door from the corridor where he was now standing.

'We're in trouble again,' Dick Barton announced. 'Get into the room next door and see if there's any way of stopping this infernal machine.'

'Right,' Snowey answered. He ducked back into the corridor.

Virginia Marley looked at Dick Barton as the spikes inched their way towards them. Her brother Rex was between them. She was terrified.

When the lights came on in the corridor of the underground complex, Jock Anderson was caught completely unawares. There was no cover anywhere.

Then, two guards came around the bend in the passage. They saw Jock and began to unsling their guns. But the mechanic was too quick for them. He had his sten gun ready. He fired a short burst and the guards toppled to the ground.

Hetherington, who was still covering Melissa with his automatic while his former co-conspirator Melganik lay dead on the floor, heard the sound of gunfire from the corridor outside and moved towards the door of the cavernous room.

'Your saboteurs have been discovered I think, Miss Agranova.'

Melissa looked at Hetherington with complete con-

111

tempt. 'You fool, Hetherington,' she hissed. 'There never were any saboteurs.'

'A likely tale,' the renegade M.P. replied. He motioned her towards him with the automatic. 'Come here.'

When Melissa had done as he had ordered, Hetherington pushed her in front of him, and moved further towards the door.

Virginia Marley and Dick Barton huddled together as the spikes advanced. Virginia's face was pale and drawn.

'Dick,' she said softly.

'What, old girl?'

'I'm frightened,' she confessed.

'Don't worry,' Dick Barton comforted her. 'Snowey'll fix it if anyone can.'

Then, as if to confirm Dick Barton's opinion of his ex-sergeant, the humming of the generator stopped, and the spikes stopped their deadly advance.

'What did I tell you?' Dick Barton said.

But then, the humming started up once more.

'No – listen,' Virginia screamed.

Even the special agent was disturbed – until he realised what was happening. 'What the . . . ' he began, and then, he broke out into a smile. 'No! Look! He's put the thing into reverse. Good old Snowey!'

With tears in her eyes, Virginia Marley watched the spikes retract into the walls. 'Oh – thank heaven,' she managed. 'Thank heaven!'

When he was sure that the two Oriental guards were dead, Jock Anderson bent down over the body of the nearest one, and began to remove the guard's revolver from his holster. His fingers had closed over the butt of the gun, when he heard a sharp English voice from behind.

'Don't move!'

Hetherington had come out of the operations room, and now, using Melissa as a shield, he pointed his automatic pistol at Jock.

'Drop the sten,' Hetherington commanded. 'I'm sure you wouldn't want to shoot a lady.'

For a moment, Jock felt that he had no real choice. He

112

didn't know who the character with the gun was, but he certainly didn't like the look of him. Rather unwillingly, he dropped the sten and backed away.

'Hands in the air!'

Jock Anderson did as he was told. And although he had seen Dick Barton appear around the corner of the corridor behind the character with the automatic, he gave no indication of the fact.

'Now – who are you? Who are you working for?'

In a second, Dick Barton sized up the situation. He signalled to Snowey and Virginia, who were coming up behind him, supporting Rex between, to stop. Then, taking his pipe from his pocket, and holding it upside down, with the bowl in his hand, he advanced silently behind Hetherington.

'Come on now,' the renegade M.P. said to Jock. 'Speak up!'

Jock Anderson stalled for time. 'Well, you see, sir . . . '

Dick Barton, who was now within striking distance, jabbed his reversed pipe into the small of Hetherington's back. 'Drop it, Hetherington,' he ordered.

The renegade M.P. was too startled to question the ruse. He dropped the automatic.

Jock Anderson was relieved, he smiled slowly as he lowered his hands.

Still holding his pipe, Dick Barton spoke to the mechanic 'Pick up his gun, will you, Jock?'

The Scotsman came forward and did as Dick Barton suggested. Hetherington had not turned around.

'Now you and the others get out of here quick while I keep these characters, covered,' Dick Barton said once Jock had picked up Hetherington's gun. He was wondering how long the deception would last, and was relying on the fact that Hetherington's fear would be conveyed to Melissa.

'What about you, Mr Barton?' Jock Anderson asked as he started down the corridor towards the spot where Virginia and Snowey were standing with Rex Marley between them. When he reached them, all four began hurrying towards the exit.

'Now – in there, you,' Dick Barton said to Hetherington

and Melissa. He prodded them towards the nearest door, opened it, pushed them in, and slammed and locked it after them. Then he turned and ran down the corridor after the others.

When Barton reached the end of the corridor that led to the main doors, he saw that Virginia, Jock and Snowey, and Rex had been stopped by the guards. They were standing just outside the main door. One of the guards, while covering them with his sten gun, was shouting questions at them in Chinese. The group looked at each other with baffled expressions.

Keeping cool, Dick Barton strode past them, guard included. He barked a few words of Chinese as he went. The effect was as he had calculated; the guards lowered their guns.

'Come on you, chaps,' Barton said. He continued striding confidently up to Melganik's car, a large American saloon.

Snowey, Jock, Virginia and Rex came towards the car. Jock recognised it at once. It was an American AS Sedan, made in 1935, not exactly the kind of machinery he loved. A bit too indulgent for his tastes. But, still, it offered a possible means of escape.

'In you get – quick,' Barton said as they approached.

They all piled into the car without hesitation. Snowey, Virginia and Rex in the back, and Jock Anderson in the passenger seat.

'I didn't know you spoke Chinese, sir,' Snowey said, as he settled into the back seat.

'Just a smattering,' came the reply. 'Accent's a bit provincial.'

Dick Barton then slid into the driver's seat and turned on the ignition.

'What did you say to them?' Jock wanted to know.

Dick Barton smiled back. 'Just, "Mr Hetherington's orders".'

'What was?' Snowey asked.

Barton grinned again as the starter motor turned and the engine caught. 'I didn't specify.' Then he put his foot

114

down on the accelerator, and the AS Sedan roared off towards the main gate.

A few minutes later, the big American car reached the narrow country road leading away from the Llanechbrantiog quarry. All the occupants were safe inside.

'Hold tight, folks,' Dick Barton remarked. 'I'm going to have to put my foot down, I'm afraid we won't have much of a start.'

Dick Barton negotiated a bend, and then accelerated once more. A quick glance in his driving mirror told him that the road was clear behind – but he couldn't see very far.

Then Snowey spoke from the back. 'We ain't got no start at all, sir, scarcely. There's the Rolls coming up behind us now.'

Jock Anderson turned and looked past Snowey, Rex, and Virginia. Through the rear window he saw the familiar pattern of the large headlights of Hetherington's 1934 Rolls Royce 20/25. 'And gaining fast!' he exclaimed.

Can Dick Barton get to London in time to warn the authorities of the imminent coup?

Or will the power of three hundred horses under the bonnet of the mighty Rolls Royce prove too much for him?

Read the next episode of: Dick Barton – Special Agent.

Chapter Ten

Barton, Snowey and Jock, having escaped from Hethering-
ton's deadly trap are speeding towards London to warn the
government of his plans for an armed takeover. Hether-
ington is hot on their trail...
Now read on.

Dick Barton kept his foot on the accelerator of the AS
Sedan. The inside of the American car was illuminated by
the Rolls Royce's headlights. They were nose to tail on the
narrow country road and there was nothing more that the
special agent could do about it. By his side, Jock Anderson's face showed up a ghastly white in the reflected headlamps of the pursuing car.

'They've got the leg on us, I'm afraid,' Dick Barton
said. 'These Yank jobs aren't built for the rolling English
road.'

The special agent didn't mention that he was behind the
wheel of a left-hand drive, that he didn't know the terri-
tory, and that in terms of engine power, they were at a
distinct disadvantage. All these he compensated for with
his driving skill.

'Never you mind about that, sir,' Jock Anderson said
confidently. He kept his eyes on the speedometer.

'What do you mean, Jock?' Dick Barton asked. 'Have
you been up to your tricks again?'

The speedometer needle on the bulky American car
touched fifty. Simultaneously, from behind, there came a
tremendous booming explosion. The AS Sedan juddered,
but Dick Barton kept it under control. Jock Anderson saw
the orange flash in the speedo glass as the Rolls Royce
20/25 caught fire. It was a sad end for such a fine piece of
machinery.

'What the dickens...' Barton exclaimed.

'Och – it was nothing, sir,' the mechanic replied modestly.

Dick Barton put his foot on the brake pedal.

When the AS Sedan stopped, the doors were flung open, and its occupants ran back along the country road. They didn't have to go very far. They soon came to a shallow, smoking crater. Scattered along the roadside were pieces of smoking scrap metal. There were fragments in the hedges, and small pieces of shattered glass littered the grass verge. That was all. There was no sign of any occupants alive or dead.

Dick Barton turned towards the mechanic. 'Jock,' he said. 'I think explanations are the order of the day.'

The Scotsman seemed to be slightly embarrassed. Hesitantly, he replied; 'Well, sir – it was just that I happened to have those sticks of rock in my pocket. Seemed a pity to waste them.'

'The dynamite they rigged up in Captain Barton's car?' Snowey chipped in after he'd finished looking at the wreckage.

'Right. So I just thought I'd give them a taste of their own jollop,' Jock replied quietly.

Dick Barton stroked his chin. It was about time he had a shave, he thought. 'Hoist with their own petard, eh?' he mused.

'Their what, sir?' Snowey wanted to know.

Barton smiled at his ex-sergeant. 'Stand easy, Snowey.'

'Oh – right you are, sir.'

It was now Virginia's time to speak. She had been standing at the edge of the group while they discussed what had happened. 'So that's the end of that,' she said with relief.

'By no means,' Dick Barton said grimly. 'Those drugged cigarettes are still going on the market, remember. We've got that to stop before we can count our chickens.'

Snowey White was keen to get the job over and done with – once and for all. 'Well, let's get moving then, sir,' he replied.

Dick Barton said one word: 'Right.' Then he began to walk back towards the car. The others followed.

*

Some hours later, the same group, with the addition of Sir Richard Marley, were standing in the book-lined study of the millionaire industrialist's home. His son Rex was slumped in an armchair. Sir Richard himself stood in front of a blazing fire and the others were ranged around the room, with Dick Barton nearest the peer.

'And that's the whole story, Sir Richard,' Barton said as he finished the tale of megalomania that had led them to Llanechbrantiog and back.

'The cold-blooded swine,' the millionaire commented.

'My sentiments exactly,' added Dick Barton.

Virginia took a stride towards her father. 'We've got to stop them, daddy,' she said anxiously. 'If those cigarettes get on to the market . . .'

Sir Richard held up his hand. 'You don't have to tell me, Virginia,' he replied. 'I've seen the victims of this scourge in my days in Egypt. Hashish smokers – the glazed eyes, the complete lack of moral fibre . . .'

Incisively, Dick Barton interrupted Sir Richard's description.

'But how do we prevent that tragedy from being enacted in this country?'

Sir Richard thought for a moment. 'The bales of tobacco were headed where?'

'The Dominion Tobacco Company,' came the crisp reply.

The name struck a chord with the industrialist. 'Didn't we build an irrigation system for them before the war, Dick?'

Barton thought for a minute. It all seemed such a long time ago. Before he had even been a captain in the commandos. 'By George,' he said after a while. 'You're right, sir!' Suddenly, it all came flooding back to him. 'Of course we did. For their plantation outside Bulawayo. I got to know young Eddie Moulton quite well out there.'

From the far end of the room, Snowey watched in amazement. Sometimes he wondered if the governor forgot anything at all. Better than a blooming elephant, he was – and much lighter on his feet.

'Moulton?' Sir Richard was looking in puzzlement at his former employee.

'The chairman's son,' Dick Barton explained. 'He was out there learning the business. He's managing director now, I believe.' Then, more directly: 'May I use your phone?'

Without waiting for Sir Richard's reply, Barton crossed the room, picked up the receiver, and began to dial.

Virginia turned to her father once again. There was an anxious look on her face. 'What are we going to do about Rex?'

The industrialist was anxious to reassure his daughter. He'd already checked with the best authorities. 'I've talked to Sir Barnett Friedmann about him. The well known physician. His opinion is that if we can keep him away from the odious stuff for two weeks . . . '

Virginia interrupted eagerly: 'He can be cured?'

'As good as new, Friedmann said,' the peer finished.

Then, as Dick Barton began to speak into the telephone, the conversation between Virginia and her father died away. No one in the well furnished room was indifferent to what information he might procure. It was a matter of life and death – of a nation.

'Eddie?' Barton asked calmly. 'Have I dragged you from your slumbers? It's Barton here – Dick Barton. Well enough, old son. You remember the raid on your bonded warehouse?' There was a pause while he waited for the voice at the other end to answer. 'Yes. When nothing appeared to be missing – right. Well something was missing – bales K26–K37.' His voice grew more serious. 'The miscreants substituted something very nasty for your doubtless excellent tobacco.' He paused again. 'Yes. I see. The whole consignment? Right. Thanks, Eddie.'

When he had replaced the telephone on the hook, Barton turned to the eagerly waiting group.

Sir Richard was the first to speak: 'What news, Dick?'

Barton's expression was grim. 'Not so good, I'm afraid.'

'What's up, sir?' Snowey asked.

'That particular consignment of tobacco has passed through their factory already,' the special agent replied flatly.

'Och – ' Jock Anderson commented loudly. 'That's awful bad, sir.'

Dick Barton glanced at the still prone Rex Marley. He hadn't moved from the couch since he'd been put there on arrival. 'It's none too bright, Jock, I grant you.'

'Do they know what brand of cigarettes the stuff went into?' Sir Richard asked.

Dick Barton now glanced questioningly at the peer. 'They do – as a matter of fact – it's their top selling cigarette – Golden Frond.

Sir Richard then strode over to the telephone and picked up the receiver. 'I think we can do something about this,' he muttered as he began to dial. Then, he spoke into the telephone. 'Give me Sir John Reigh, please.'

Snowey White wondered what was going on. He looked across to where the governor was standing, but he seemed happy enough. Snowey shrugged his shoulders.

The next day, in the studio of Broadcasting House, a radio announcer sat at his desk as a special bulletin was brought in. The red light flashed. He looked down at the bulletin and began to read. It was a nationwide broadcast at peak listening time.

'This is the BBC Home and Forces programme,' the announcer said. *'Here is the news. In a special warning today the police have asked the public to return to their retailer . . . '*

The airwaves hummed as the message was transmitted from relay station to relay station.

' . . . Any packets of Golden Frond cigarettes which they may have purchased this morning . . . '

In a perfectly ordinary room in a typical house in the North of England, a man put a cigarette in his mouth. Then, the warning continued on the radio.

' . . . retailers have been authorised to refund the complete purchase price . . . '

As the announcer's voice crackled through the static, the man put down the box of matches he held in his hand. Then, he looked down at the packet of cigarettes he was still holding. The brand name was Golden Frond.

And, in a well to do, expensively furnished apartment in

120

Kensington, a well dressed woman looked down at the packet of the same cigarettes that was lying next to the radio on a specially built corner shelf.

' . . . this is due to a toxic substance having been introduced into a batch of the cigarettes by criminal elements.'

The woman turned the radio off and stared at her packet of Golden Frond.

At the same time, on a country road that eventually led to London, one of the army trucks from Llanechbrantiog quarry was flagged down at the barrier manned by the regular forces.

Dick Barton, standing at the side of the road with an army officer, smiled with satisfaction as a Black Maria reversed out of a side road up to the back of the army truck.

Two private soldiers and a sergeant ordered the occupants of the truck, a dozen Orientals from Hetherington's private army, out of the vehicle. Then they made them discard their arms into a pile on the road.

As the Chinese were forced into the Black Maria, the Special Agent smiled once more.

It was exactly a fortnight later. Dick Barton, Jock, Snowey, Sir Richard and Virginia sat at a large table at the edge of the dance floor in the Mayfair club known as the *Blue Parrot*. On stage, a trio was playing, it was the same band that had been there on the previous occasion.

It was a happier event, this time, Dick Barton thought, as he finished telling the others about the way they had rounded up all Hetherington's private army. 'So that was the end of that little attempt at a coup d'état,' he concluded.

Snowey looked across to his governor. 'Blooming good job too, sir, if you ask me,' he commented.

Sir Richard took another sip of his champagne. 'That sort of thing won't wash in this country, thank the lord,' he said.

Virginia looked admiringly around the table. 'Certainly not while there are fellows like Mr Barton, and Snowey

121

about,' she complimented them.

'What about wee Jock Anderson?' the mechanic asked with mock dismay.

Virginia laughed in reply. 'And you, Jock, of course – I'm sorry.'

Sir Richard put down his glass and leant across the table. There was a sterner expression on his face. 'But seriously,' he began. 'We may have won the war but there's a new war to be fought now. The fight against complaisancy – the fight against immorality.'

'And the war against evil men like Charles Hetherington,' Virginia added excitedly.

'Right,' Snowey White agreed.

When Dick Barton spoke, it was with some deliberation. This had been a matter that had been on his mind for some time. 'It's odd – your average Englishman, well, he may be a bit stolid – a bit slow to take offence – not the cleverest johnny in the world – but there's a streak of decency – just plain, ordinary decency – that runs right through him.' He paused while the others listened closely. 'I mean, he doesn't believe that might is right or any of that nonsense – but when his back's to the wall he'll fight like a tiger.' The figure of Charles Hetherington, renegade M.P., crossed his mind. 'But then again we seem to throw up occasionally, don't we, the odd real bad hat. And when an Englishman goes to the bad it's just about the rottenest sight you could hope not to see.'

'I second that,' Jock Anderson cut in quickly.

There was laughter all around the table.

Barton grinned at Jock: 'Of course, a Scot never goes to the bad, I suppose.'

'You're darned right,' Jock agreed.

It was Snowey White's turn to comment: 'Haggis-addicts one and all,' he quipped.

When the laughter died down, Sir Richard turned towards the special agent. Once more, his tone was serious. 'But what about you, Dick? That job's still open for you, you know.'

The events concerned with the renegade Hetherington and the master criminal had decided Dick Barton in one direction. 'I know sir, and don't think I'm not grateful,' he replied. 'But . . . '

Sir Richard raised his hand. ' 'Nuff said, Dick.'

Then, there was a roll of drums and crash of cymbals from the stage. They all turned in that direction. Sam, the manager of the *Blue Parrot*, was standing at the microphone in the middle of a spotlight.

'And now, ladies and gentlemen,' he announced. 'It's cabaret time at the *Blue Parrot*.' He was looking much happier than he'd been the last time they'd met, Dick Barton thought. 'And I'd like you to give an especially warm welcome to someone who's now recovered from the serious illness that forced him to leave the stage at his last performance in our club,' Sam continued. 'That star of stage, screen and radio – Mr Rex Marley!'

The manager looked towards the wing, the trio struck up Rex Marley's theme tune, and the crooner himself strode on to the stage. He was looking fit and happy, and very confident. The trio then swung into an up-tempo version of *Blue Skies* and Rex came in right on time. His singing was superb.

Dick Barton turned towards Virginia. 'Well,' he remarked. 'Your brother's really swinging tonight.'

Virginia glanced towards the stage, and then smiled at the Special Agent. She nodded and said: 'Really cooking with gas.'

There were smiles of enjoyment all around the table. The atmosphere in the club was becoming excited. Virginia couldn't help noticing that her father was tapping his foot under the table.

Some hours later, the floorshow had finished, the bar was shut and the club was getting ready to close. Waiters were moving around the room, upending chairs on to the tables. In the corner, Sam looked at his watch and then dimmed the lights. Dick Barton, Snowey and Jock were the only customers left. They weren't eating. Or drinking. Or even smoking. They just didn't want everything to end.

'Hm,' Dick Barton remarked after a while.

'Aye,' Jock said.

'One for the road?' Snowey suggested.

Jock Anderson shook his head. 'I've a long walk home.'

Snowey looked quizzically at the Scotsman. 'What're you talking about?'

'Walk?' Dick Barton also thought it was odd.

'I've missed my last bus,' Jock explained.

Snowey leant back in his chair. 'But from here to your place . . . blimey mate. That's not a walk, it's a blooming safari.'

Jock glanced around the room, the manager was now obviously impatient for them to leave. He saw Sam look at his watch again. 'It's not so bad,' Jock said after a while.

'Nonsense,' Dick Barton declared. 'We'll run you home in the car.' He got up to go. Snowey and Jock followed.

The Riley Monaco went quietly through the London streets. It was late, there was no one about. The street lamps cast pools of light on the glistening road surface. It must have rained quite recently, Dick Barton thought as he drove in silence. From the back of the car, he heard Snowey yawn fitfully. Jock Anderson stirred in the passenger seat.

'Funny,' Jock said slowly. 'You get caught up with people and all of a sudden –' he snapped his fingers expressively. 'That's all.'

Dick Barton gave the Scots mechanic a quick glance. 'It wasn't all fun,' he said.

'You can say that again,' Snowey agreed from the back of the car.

Jock shifted in his seat again. 'No,' he replied. 'But somehow . . . I don't know. We were all in it together.'

'Like the war,' Snowey added.

There was silence for a while. 'In a way that was the best thing about it,' the Special Agent commented.

'Right,' Snowey said.

Barton glanced towards the others again. 'How would you two feel about us sticking together?'

'Man, I'd like that fine,' Jock replied feelingly.

'Me and all,' said Snowey. 'Doing what, though?'

'Same sort of thing,' Dick Barton turned a corner. He was now about three streets away from where Jock lived.

'Getting decent types out of a hole. Fighting . . . well, wrong. I'm willing to stake the rest of my gratuity on seeing how it works out.'

'I'm with you,' Jock said immediately. There was a smile on his face. He felt relieved.

'You know me,' Snowey chipped in. 'Try anything once.'

'Good show,' said the special agent. 'Then let's meet and talk about it. My place. Say eleven ack emma.'

They were now at the corner of Jock's street, Dick Barton slowed the Riley and brought it to a stop outside a tobacconist's shop with the shutters up. Jock got out.

'See you in the morning then,' the mechanic said, as he closed the car door and began to walk towards his house. 'Thanks for the lift.'

'Not a bit. Goodnight.' Dick Barton noticed that the Riley was idling evenly. A useful man, Jock, he thought.

'Goodnight sir,' Jock turned and lingered for a moment on the pavement. 'Snowey.'

The ex-sergeant leant forward and called out of the window. 'Jock,' he acknowledged.

This time Jock began to walk without hesitation towards his house. Snowey watched him go. Dick Barton put the Riley into gear, and was about to move off again.

Suddenly, Snowey stiffened in his seat. 'Hang about, sir,' he said.

He pointed to further down the street. A girl wearing a raincoat and headscarf was waving at Jock.

'Mr Anderson!'

Snowey and Dick Barton watched as Jock turned uncertainly towards the girl. It was obvious that he didn't recognise her. But she continued to approach him, holding a piece of paper in her hand. Then, the shadowy figure of a man, dressed in a trenchcoat and trilby, broke from the darkness. The girl saw him and began to run. The man pursued her.

'Come on,' Dick Barton shouted. He and Snowey leapt out of the car as the man in the trenchcoat caught up with the girl, smashing her to the ground as he tried to prise the paper from her hand.

'Here!'

125

Jock Anderson, realising that, whoever they both were, the man in the trenchcoat was obviously up to no good, began to run towards them.

The man looked up. Seeing three figures approach from two different directions, he gave up his attempt and began to run down the street.

'Get him, Snowey!'

Snowey raced after the fleeing bully while Barton and Jock tended the unconscious girl. The Special Agent frowned as he bent over her. He never had liked a man who attacked women. He hoped the girl's injury wasn't too serious.

After a minute or so, Snowey White came back. He was panting. 'Lost him,' he said. 'It's a blooming rabbit warren down there.'

Barton indicated the unconscious girl. 'She'll live,' he announced. Then, he turned to Jock. 'Who is she?'

'I've no idea,' the mechanic admitted.

'What's that in her hand?' Snowey asked.

Jock reached across, took the piece of paper that was still held in the unconscious girl's hand, and smoothed it out. 'Good God,' he said slowly.

The special agent had no difficulty in recognising it. 'It looks like half of a British Army of Occupation banknote,' he said.

'Funny money,' Snowey White commented.

Then, they both watched as Jock Anderson reached into the inside pocket of his jacket. He brought out his wallet, and from it, he extracted his own piece of paper. He placed it against the other half. It matched exactly.

'All done by mirrors,' Snowey continued.

Barton looked towards Jock once more. 'What's the story?'

Jock Anderson looked down at the girl, then at the matching pieces of paper. 'George Cameron was my officer in the war. I saved his life once. He returned the compliment. When we were demobbed, we, like, tore this in half,' he indicated the banknote. 'If either of us ever got into trouble he'd only to send his half to the other . . . ' Jock's voice trailed off as he looked down at the girl again. He still didn't recognise her.

'Better get her under cover and let the quack have a look at that crack on her napper,' Snowey declared.

'My landlady'd have kittens,' Jock said.

But Dick Barton had already made up his mind, even though he didn't know where all this might lead. 'Let's get her into the car,' he said crisply.

Snowey smiled ruefully at his governor. 'Another night on the couch for guess who?'

'It looks like we're back in business,' Jock Anderson said as Dick Barton and Snowey began to carry the unconscious girl towards the Riley Monaco. He didn't sound unhappy.

Why has George Cameron appealed to Jock for help?

Who is the mystery girl and who attacked her?

Now read The Mystery of the Missing Formula – the next novel in the Dick Barton – Special Agent – series.

Wyndham Books are obtainable from many booksellers and newsagents. If you have any difficulty please send purchase price plus postage on the scale below to:

Wyndham Cash Sales:
P O Box 11,
Falmouth,
Cornwall.

or

Star Book Service:
G P O Box 29,
Douglas,
Isle of Man,
British Isles.

While every effort is made to keep prices low, it is sometimes necessary to increase prices at short notice. Wyndham Books reserve the right to show new retail prices on covers which may differ from those advertised in the text or elsewhere.

Postage and Packing Rate
UK
22p for the first book plus 10p per copy for each additional book ordered to a maximum charge of 82p.

BFPO and Eire
22p for the first book, plus 10p per copy for the next 6 books and thereafter 4p per book.

Overseas
30p for the first book and 10p per copy for each additional book.

These charges are subject to Post Office charge fluctuations.